Lost in the Storm

Lost in the Storm

Holly Webb

Illustrated by Sophy Williams

Stripes

For Tom ~ H W

Chapter One

Fluff the kitten was lying in her basket on her back, showing off her furry tummy and snoring a little. She wasn't deeply asleep, just dozing, with her paws tucked under her chin. Her little body only took up one corner of the basket. Fluff was getting bigger, just not very fast. The basket was in a patch of winter sunshine, and it was deliciously cosy. She was planning to spend as much of the afternoon as possible like this. She needed to keep her energy up, after all, for when Ella got home from school and wanted to play.

Ella's mum walked past, and Fluff opened one eye thoughtfully. Was there any chance of a snack? Ella's mum reached down to tickle her behind the ears. She hadn't wanted Ella to have a cat at first. When she and Ella first met Fluff at the farm where she'd been born, Mum had called Fluff a dirty, scruffy little kitten, and told Ella she could have a goldfish instead. (Fluff was a little sad that Ella didn't have a goldfish, actually. *She* would have liked one.) But when she'd seen how upset

Ella was, and understood that she really was old enough to look after a kitten properly, she'd changed her mind. Now she fussed over Fluff almost as much as Ella did. Fluff purred at the attention, and waved her paws idly. Ella's mum stroked the silky fur on Fluff's tummy, and laughed. She reached for the packet of cat treats on the counter. Fluff sprang out of her basket in half a second, standing on tiptoe with her paws against the cupboard door, scrabbling to get closer.

"I shouldn't be doing this." Mum shook her head. "You eat far too many of these. You'll get too big for your basket."

Fluff delicately nibbled the prawn-flavoured treat out of Mum's hand, and pranced back to her basket. She knew Ella's mum was joking. The basket was huge! Fluff liked to lie up against one edge of it, to make it seem a bit smaller. She had a feeling that Ella and her dad had gone a bit over the top in the pet shop.

After Fluff had run away from the farm to escape being taken home by a horrible boy who wanted to feed her to next door's German shepherd dog, Ella and her family had finally found her again a couple of days before Christmas. It had been the snowiest Christmas for twenty years, so Ella hadn't been able to go out and buy Fluff a Christmas present. She'd made up for it when the snow thawed, spending most of her Christmas money from Grandma on cat toys. Ella walked past a pet shop on her way home from school, and she liked to pop in and spend her pocket money on things for Fluff. Fluff didn't mind at all – she was *very* fond of those prawn-flavoured cat treats…

Suddenly, Fluff pricked up her ears. She could hear someone opening the front door. Ella was back from school!

"I'm home!" Ella called, and Fluff bounded up to the front door to twine herself round Ella's legs lovingly. She enjoyed having a nice sniff of the outdoors as well, poking her nose round the edge of the door.

Ella scooped her up gently. "Hey! No running off, Fluff!"

Fluff rubbed her head up and down Ella's chin. She wasn't trying to run off. It would just be fun to go and have a wander around outside. She hadn't been allowed out much since Ella and her family had adopted her, and sometimes it could be a little bit boring, being an indoor cat. Ella took her out in the garden at the weekends, but it was too dark when she got home from school. Fluff loved the garden, scratching the tree bark, chasing leaves, watching the bird table. She wished she could go and explore more when they were out, but she could see how worried Ella was about her getting lost again, so she stayed close by. Fluff thought it was a bit silly though – as if she could get lost by just investigating next door's garden! She'd only been lost before because she had been so young. She was a bit bigger now, and she could find her way anywhere, she was sure.

"I brought you home a present!" Ella said, as she shut the door. She carried Fluff into the kitchen, gave her mum a quick hug, and started to root around in her school bag.

"*Another* trip to the pet shop?" Mum asked, half-annoyed, half-laughing. "That cat is going to think it's Christmas every day."

Ella looked a little guilty. The pet shop was on her way home from school, and she was allowed to pop in, as long as she didn't take long. Mum liked to know where she was. "I know. But you did say she needed a collar. They haven't had any really nice ones before, but look at this!" She held up a beautiful blue leather collar. "Isn't it gorgeous? And look, it's got a place for her name and everything." She fastened it round Fluff's neck, and Fluff shook her head briskly, not sure about this new feeling.

"It's a bit big," Ella said, studying it thoughtfully. "But I suppose she'll grow into it, won't she? It looks beautiful." Dangling from the collar was a little round golden tag. "You could choose," Ella explained. "If I go back to the shop they can put her name on it. But I wanted to check what else we should put. Should we have our address engraved on it as well, in case she gets lost?"

Mum looked thoughtful for a moment. "Actually, I think just our phone number. Not even her name. I know it sounds silly, but if we put her name on, it means everyone knows it, and someone could call her over. We don't want anyone to find it easy to steal our gorgeous kitten, do we?"

Ella looked horrified. "No! I didn't think of that. Just the phone number then." She picked Fluff up again and held her tight, so tight that Fluff wriggled after a few seconds, trying to get down.

"Hey! Ella, it's OK. It's just a safety thing. It's really, really unlikely." Mum gave her an anxious look. "I know you love Fluff, and of course we don't want to lose her, but I think you're just worrying too much. Fluff's growing up now, and cats are very independent. I think you're going to have to let her out on her own soon."

Ella looked down at Fluff, who was now sniffing at the counter, hoping for more treats. "But what if she gets lost again?" she asked.

Mum sat down next to her. "There's no reason why she should, Ella. Cats have a really good sense of direction. She won't just go running off for no reason, she'll look around, make sure she knows how to get back. She's clever, isn't she?"

Ella nodded. "Yes," she agreed, and then she added doubtfully, "but she was lost before."

"She was really little then, and it wasn't her fault, anyway. She'd never been away from the farm. And she found you, didn't she? That shows you just how amazing her instincts are."

"Mmm." It was true. They'd never understood how Fluff had found her way back to them, but Ella couldn't believe it was just a coincidence.

"I think we ought to get Dad to put a cat flap in the back door. Then Fluff will be able to come in and out when she wants to."

"OK," Ella agreed reluctantly, still anxiously eyeing Fluff. She was such a small kitten, even now she'd grown a bit – and even with her podgy cat-treat-filled tummy. Would she really be safe out on her own?

At the weekend, Ella's dad went with her to the pet shop to buy Fluff a cat flap. It was the first time that Ella had been there and not enjoyed it. Normally she just wandered round wishing she had more money to buy presents for Fluff! Now she stared worriedly at the display of collars while

Dad and the pet shop owner discussed different sorts of cat flap. The engraved disk for Fluff's collar was ready for them to pick up, too, but Ella's excitement about it was almost gone. It had been replaced by a sense of relief that when Fluff went out of her new cat flap and disappeared, at least there was a chance that someone would find her and call.

The cat flap was a clever one that could be locked, or set so Fluff could only go through it one way. It was a pain to fit, though. Ella's dad had to saw a chunk out of the back door, and it took him ages. When it was finally finished, Ella crouched on the lawn waving the prawn-flavoured cat treats to tempt Fluff through. It didn't take her long to get the idea, although she looked very surprised when she first tried it. She had her front legs on the doorstep and her back legs in the kitchen, and she wasn't quite sure where her tummy was. She gave a panicked sort of wriggle, and suddenly all of her was in the garden. Fluff looked round suspiciously, not entirely sure how it had happened.

"Clever Fluff," Ella whispered, rewarding her with cat treats. "Do you like your new cat flap, mmm? You will be careful though, won't you?" She scratched Fluff's favourite behind-the-ears spot. "You stay close to the garden." Ella gulped. "No running out into the road, Fluff!"

Fluff purred as Ella petted her. She wasn't sure she completely understood this cat flap business yet, but it seemed to mean that she could just go out whenever she wanted to! And then get back in again for a snooze in her basket – it sounded brilliant to her, but she could hear in Ella's voice that she wasn't completely happy about it. She rubbed herself all round Ella twice in a comforting way, making her giggle. *I won't run away*, she promised. *Don't worry.*

For the first few days, Fluff kept her expeditions confined to the garden. There was plenty to explore there anyway. Ella had quite a big garden, long and narrow. Her mum loved gardening, and there were big flower beds, which Fluff wasn't much interested in, but also lots of exciting corners and pockets. Best of all was a tall old apple tree, its branches starting quite low to the ground. Ella had a swing in it, which she loved to sit and daydream on. The apple tree was Fluff's first real chance to practise climbing, and it made a brilliant claw-sharpener, too.

But after a little while, Fluff had found all the interesting things in her garden, and she scrambled up the fence to look down at next door. She'd seen Mrs Jones, Ella's neighbour, before. Ella had held Fluff up to the fence to be admired, and Mrs Jones had commented on her beautiful markings. Fluff hadn't had a chance to see much of the garden, but now she noticed something very exciting. She plunged down the other side of the fence with an undignified scrabble of claws, and stopped at the bottom for a calming lick of her ruffled fur. Then she set off to investigate. Mrs Jones's garden had a pond! With fish in it, Fluff soon discovered. She whiled away the rest of the afternoon perched on the rocks by the side of the water, dreamily watching the fish darting to and fro. Was it her imagination, or were they swimming slightly faster, looking a little more worried? Obviously she would need practice, but Fluff was fairly sure that if she dipped a paw in and held it still, she would be able to catch a fish…

Fluff was so interested in the fish that she almost forgot to get back to the house before Ella arrived home from school. She didn't want Ella to worry that she'd got lost, and of course, she loved to see her. She could always tell when it was nearly time for Ella to be back.

Fluff sprang up from her place on the rocks, and scooted halfway up Mrs Jones's fence before she'd even realized she was climbing. Then she nearly slid backwards, and had to jab her claws in hard to stay on. Embarrassed, she flung herself up and over and streaked across the lawn to the cat flap. Ella was just coming in the front door, and Mum laughed as Fluff shot through the flap.

"Just in time, Fluff! Oh, you're all out of breath."

Fluff glared up at her, and sat down in the middle of the kitchen floor, curling her tail round her legs in a dignified pose. She was trying not to look like a kitten who'd nearly fallen off a fence, but her whiskers were still twitchy with excitement. Outside might be a bit dangerous, but she did love it!

Chapter Two

It was mid-February, and it had suddenly got cold again. Ella was extra-glad to have Fluff sleeping on her feet at night. Mum and Dad had said that she was supposed to sleep in her basket, but they pretended not to notice that actually she always curled up with Ella. Mostly she stayed at the end of the bed, but a couple of times Ella had

gone to sleep cuddling her, and Fluff
slept snuggled under her chin.

Ella woke up early that morning.
The duvet was huddled up around
her shoulders where she'd wriggled
herself down in the cold of the night.
Fluff was pacing up and down the
window sill, mewing excitedly.

"Fluff!" Ella moaned. "It's not even properly light yet, what's the matter?" Then she sat up, confused. It was almost light, but the room looked different somehow. And why was Fluff making such a fuss? Ella wrapped the duvet round her shoulders like a cloak and padded over to the window.

"Oh, wow! It's snowed again!" she exclaimed as she peered out.

It had snowed very heavily just before Christmas, when Fluff was lost, but the cold snap hadn't lasted long. January had just been grim and wet.

"Why does it have to be a school day?" Ella sighed. "It'll be too dark to play outside much after school."

Ella tried to argue at breakfast that school would probably be closed because of the snow, but Mum said it would have been announced on the radio. She promised faithfully to help Ella build an entire family of snowmen when she got back, and they dug out wellies and scarves and hats for the walk. Ella normally walked on her own to school. It wasn't very far, and she met up with lots of her friends, but today Mum said she'd go too, at least most of the way, because she was worried Ella might slip over in the snow.

"Don't go out today, Fluff," Ella said, as she struggled to pull her wellies on over two pairs of socks. "It's really cold, and the snow's very deep. You'd probably sink up to your whiskers. Stay in the house and keep nice and warm."

Fluff snuggled into her basket and snoozed for a while, but she was itching to go outside. Despite what Ella had said, Fluff really wanted to investigate the snow. She padded over to the cat flap and peered out. The snow was brand new and inviting. She couldn't see any tracks in it, just a sheet of crunchy, sparkling white. She pushed the cat flap open gently with her nose, and sniffed. The snow smelled so fresh, and she could hear the wind blowing through the trees, the snow falling from the branches with soft *whumpf* noises. How could she stay inside? She wouldn't go far...

Fluff eased herself out of the cat flap, shaking her paws daintily as they hit the snow. She knew all about snow, of course. Her long journey from the farm to Ella's house had nearly ended in disaster when she was caught in a snowstorm. But today she was just going for a quick look around. Nothing could go wrong. She'd explore the snowy garden, and as soon as she felt cold or tired, she could go back inside to warm up, and probably beg some cat treats from Ella's mum. Ella was just being too careful, Fluff thought. It was nice that Ella wanted to look after her, but really, she could look after herself!

Fluff's paws sank deeply into the snow. It must have been snowing for most of the night, as there was a thick layer over everything. The garden looked completely different, covered in strange lumps where the plants had been. Fluff looked down and saw her paw prints in the snow – the only ones. It was very exciting to be the only animal outside. She gave a little jump to make more prints, scattering her tracks around the lawn in a pattern.

It was still snowing a little, the flakes drifting down idly, tickling Fluff's whiskers. She sat up on her back legs and tried to catch them with her front paws, but the snowflakes floated on the wind, and it was hard to tell where they were going. One particularly large flake came twirling down past Fluff's nose, and she whisked her paws at it. It seemed to dodge, she twirled around to chase it and suddenly she was flat on her tummy in the snow. Fluff stood up quickly, checking that no one had seen her slide. The snowflake had disappeared into the thousands of other snowflakes, and Fluff spat snow out of her mouth crossly. She plunged off across the garden to find something else to do.

Suddenly she noticed that hers weren't the only tracks any more. A delicate pattern of forked prints was spattered over the snow by the fence. And perched on top of the fence, eyeing her cautiously, was a blackbird!

It whistled shrilly and hopped down into the next-door garden. Fluff trotted along the path of tracks eagerly. She'd got the hang of walking in the snow again now, lifting her paws higher than usual. The tracks led underneath the fence, and Fluff wriggled after them, not even remembering that she'd planned to stay in her own garden. The blackbird was on the bird table now, gobbling breadcrumbs that she'd put out. It must have been that morning, because Fluff could see the prints of Mrs Jones's wellies in the snow. She gazed hopefully up at the blackbird for a while, but it just squawked and chattered at her angrily. Clearly it didn't fancy coming down to be chased.

She hopped from footprint to footprint instead, and realized that Mrs Jones must have gone down to check on the pond as well. Her prints led right up to the edge. Fluff stood in them and leaned over to look. The pond was frozen! She could see the water-plants poking out in places, snow drifted up around them, but most of the pond was covered with strange, clear, greenish ice. Fluff couldn't see the fish at all, they must be hiding away at the bottom. Cautiously, she put a paw on the ice, and it skidded. She jumped back quickly. She'd already fallen over once, and the ice was horribly cold.

The pond was close to Mrs Jones's fence, and there was an inviting gap underneath. The next garden smelled really interesting; somehow the cold was making all the smells so much better! Fluff flattened herself to the ground and squirmed through the gap, her whiskers twitching excitedly. Then she squirmed some more, and then she wriggled. Then she stopped wriggling. She wasn't going anywhere. She was stuck!

Chapter Three

Fluff hunched her shoulders worriedly, trying to work out what had gone wrong. The gap had looked perfectly big enough – her whiskers had fitted through, so the rest of her should have been able to. Then she realized – it was her collar. It had caught on something, maybe a nail sticking out of the fence. Suddenly Fluff panicked and started to struggle, pulling backwards and forwards desperately, mewing frantically and scrabbling with her paws. She mewed for Ella to come and help her, forgetting that Ella was at school. But after a couple of minutes she was too exhausted to struggle any longer, and she slumped to the ground, her neck aching where the collar was pulling at her.

Fluff lay panting miserably, wondering what to do. She supposed she would just have to wait for someone to rescue her. When she didn't get home in time to meet Ella from school, they would start to worry, wouldn't they? Or maybe Mrs Jones would come out to look at her pond again. Fluff shivered. It was going to be a horribly long, cold wait.

Fluff mewed with frustration. It was just so stupid. Her collar was too big, and it had got caught. It wasn't her fault! She gave a furious wriggle, and suddenly felt the collar stretch. Perhaps instead of trying to pull the collar off the fence, she should be trying to get out of the collar altogether. She pulled downwards, trying to stretch the collar even more. It hurt a bit, but the collar did seem to give. Now if she could just pull herself backwards…

Fluff popped out of the collar, feeling as though she might have pulled her ears off. She twitched them. No, they were still there. She'd done it! Feeling very proud of herself, she examined the collar. There wasn't a nail, just a sharp splinter of wood sticking out of the fence. Fluff hadn't been as far as the next garden on her travels before, so as she came out from under the fence she looked around carefully, trying to work out if this was another cat's territory, or even worse, if there was a dog around. Everything smelled all right, but she wasn't sure how the snow changed smells, and she wanted to be extra cautious. As she sat watching, she noticed a strange metal thing in the middle of the garden, a pole, with things hanging from it. Fluff sat with her head on one side, trying to work out what it might be. Suddenly two birds flew down to perch on the hanging bits, and she realized it was full of birdseed. Fluff's ears pricked forward, and she sank into a hunting crouch. If only she could get closer... Fluff hadn't had much opportunity to practise her hunting skills yet, but she was keen to learn. Her mother had tried to teach her how to catch mice back at the farm, but Fluff thought birds looked more fun to chase.

With a heavy flumping sound, a pair of enormously fat wood pigeons thumped down on to the snowy grass. They were too big to perch on the feeders, but there were a few bits of seed and nuts scattered about in the snow underneath, and the pigeons set to gobbling them up greedily.

Fluff's heart began to beat faster with excitement. This was her chance! How pleased Ella would be if Fluff brought her back a pigeon! She left her hiding place and crawled closer on her tummy, low to the ground, her paws muffled by the snow. The pigeons completely ignored her, too busy making sure they didn't miss any bits of seed that might be half-buried in the snow. With a massive burst of energy, Fluff pounced, fastening her teeth into the tail of the nearest pigeon, which let out a loud squawk of surprise. She'd done it! She'd actually caught something!

The pigeon looked round, saw that it was being attacked by a cat in the middle of its lunch, and panicked. All right, so it was only a very small cat, but then pigeons are known for having very small brains.

Squawking in horror, the pigeon tried to fly away, but this was a bit difficult with a cat attached to a vital part of its flying equipment. Fluff hung on grimly as the wings beat up and down. Her first catch was *not* getting away. Seeing that flapping wasn't going to work, the pigeon changed its tactics, and began to run *and* flap, trying to build up some speed to help lift itself off the ground. Rather like a feathery plane thundering down the runway, it set off across the lawn. Fluff was dragged along behind like a waterskier, her paws making great tracks in the snow.

At last the pigeon managed enough lift and pulled itself off the ground with a mighty effort, taking Fluff with it. Her front paws left the ground, and she peered down worriedly. Surely the pigeon couldn't actually fly off with her... There was no way she was going to let go! Luckily for Fluff, the tail gave up instead. A great clump of feathers came right out, and the pigeon flew off looking decidedly bald. It landed clumsily at the top of a nearby tree, and squawked abuse at Fluff, furiously preening its mangled tail. Fluff sat on the ground, panting and spitting feathers. Did that count as catching a pigeon? she wondered. Could she claim it as half a pigeon, perhaps? She heaved a happy sigh, and spat out a last feather.

Fluff gazed up at the pigeon, still angrily squawking at her, and noticed that it had started to snow again. She danced around the lawn, pouncing on the twirling snowflakes. This was so much fun! It was cold, of course, but her thick fur was keeping her cosy, and in a few minutes she would head back to her cat flap and the lovely warm house. She chased round and round, whisking her tail, still full of excitement after her hunt. The snow was coming in big, thick flakes now, large enough to snap at with her teeth.

Fluff was enjoying herself so much that she didn't notice how heavy the snow was becoming. The pigeons and the other birds had disappeared, and it was terribly quiet. Fluff opened her mouth and tried to catch a particularly plump and dizzy snowflake, and then looked around in surprise. She couldn't see! The whole garden was a mass of whirling white and grey, and Fluff couldn't see anything beyond two whisker-lengths away. She shuddered. This was too much like her scary journey a couple of months before. She needed to get home at once. But – where was home? Fluff gulped. She couldn't even see the fence.

A gust of icy wind rushed at Fluff, and she felt as though it had blown right through her. Her ears were laid back against her head, and the snowflakes felt like stabbing needles as they blew into her fur.

Worriedly, she peered around her. She could just about see the tree that the pigeon had flown into, so the fence must be over there somewhere. Leaning into the wind, she ploughed forward. It was so cold now! Oh, at last, there was the fence. Fluff's panicky feeling eased a little. She only had to get across next-door's garden and she would be home. She wriggled under the fence, and then followed her nose straight across. She was nearly there – and once she was back home, she was *not* coming out again. Not till it stopped snowing, anyway.

Fluff almost bumped into the next fence, but she didn't mind, she was just so glad to see it. She popped out from underneath; she was back in her garden!

Except – this didn't look like her garden. Even with the snow everywhere, it didn't feel right. Ella's garden had lots of little walls and hedges and things, but this garden was big and flat. Had she miscounted the number of fences? Fluff didn't think she'd gone into another garden after next-door-but-one, but perhaps in the excitement of exploring, she had...?

Feeling frightened, she scurried across this strange garden to the next fence, hoping desperately that this time she would see somewhere she knew. The snow was drifting up against the fences now, and she had to half-burrow through. Hopefully, she pushed the snow out of the way with her nose, and stared around. This garden was full of play equipment, a slide and a little wooden house, half covered in snow. Fluff had never been here before.

Fluff had gone the wrong way in the storm – and now she was completely lost!

Chapter Four

Fluff stood still for a while, sniffing the air, hoping to catch a familiar scent that would lead her home. But the snow deadened the smells as well as the noises, and Fluff felt completely blind. What should she do? Had she gone past Ella's house in the storm somehow? Should she be going back or forwards?

One thing was certain. She *had* to move somewhere. Sitting still wouldn't keep her warm. She could feel the cold seeping into her bones – even her whiskers ached with it. The awful thing was, she might be going even further away from home! Miserably, Fluff forced her paws to keep plodding on through the deep snow. Without realizing, she slipped through a gap in a broken-down old fence at the bottom of a garden, and strayed into the old wood that ran along behind the houses on Ella's street. It was even harder going. She was wading through drifted snow under tall and menacing trees. Fluff knew she'd never been anywhere like this before, and it made her shudder. The trees seemed to wave their dark arms at her, and their roots tripped her up. It felt as though they did it on purpose, sending her rolling into hollows of deep snow, so she had to struggle and fight her way out. Every time it happened, Fluff grew just a little bit more tired.

It was getting dark, and even harder to see. Fluff wished sadly that she had listened to Ella, and never gone out in the snow. She still didn't quite understand how she had managed to get so lost. One minute she had known exactly where she was, and the next she'd had no idea. It had all happened so fast. Fluff shivered. There was nothing she could do about it now. She needed to rest, but where could she go? There were a few places under the trees, where the roots had made little burrows, but they didn't look very warm. Fluff needed somewhere out of the biting wind.

Suddenly, something loomed up out of the gloom. Fluff peered forward doubtfully. It certainly wasn't a tree. In fact, it looked more like a house.

With a fresh burst of energy, she trotted forward, picking her way carefully over the snow. It was a tumbledown old cottage, built for the gamekeeper who guarded the wood, but it had been empty now for years and years. The door was boarded up, but there were plenty of holes where a small cat could creep in. Fluff sighed with relief as she squeezed herself between the boards. Even just inside the door the difference was wonderful – no more freezing wind slicing through her fur.

Staggering with tiredness, Fluff headed further in, looking for somewhere comfortable to sleep. Gratefully she spotted a pile of old blankets in one corner. They were smelly and stained, but Fluff wasn't feeling fussy. She burrowed in, wanting to be as warm as possible, and hollowed herself out a little nest in the rags. She closed her eyes, wrapped her tail round her nose, and let a warm tide of sleep wash over her. All at once she was back home, with Ella, being stroked, and fed cat treats.

But then she heard a noise. Fluff twitched in her sleep, fighting to stay in her lovely dream. Oh, she didn't *want* to wake up, and be back in this cold, real adventure! Something was breaking into her dream – a mewing sound. Fluff sighed. It was no good, she wasn't asleep any more. She poked her head up from her blanket nest, and gazed round grumpily. She couldn't see anything, and the cottage was silent, except for the eerie shrieking of the wind outside. Was it that she'd heard? It must have been. Fluff was just settling back down to sleep when she heard the mewing again.

Something was crying for help!

Ella rushed home – as fast as she could in slippery wellies – full of news about her fun day. School had been all about snow – talking about snowflake patterns in science, writing snow poems in English, and lots and lots of playing outside in the snow at lunch and break.

"We had a brilliant snowball fight," Ella told her mum happily, as she watched her make a mug of hot chocolate. "Oooh, can I have marshmallows, please? Excellent." She took the chocolate and sat down, sipping it slowly. "Yum. It's so cold out there, Mum, my fingers are freezing, even though I had my gloves on." She gripped the warm mug tightly. "They're only just thawing out." Ella took a big mouthful of chocolate, and sighed happily. It was nice to be back inside. "It's so cool that it's Friday, and we've got the whole weekend free. Can we go sledging in the park tomorrow?" Then she looked round, suddenly realizing that she hadn't seen Fluff since she got back. "Mum, where's Fluff? She didn't go out, did she?" Ella asked anxiously.

Her mum looked surprised. "But she's got her cat flap now, Ella, she's allowed outside! I saw her playing in the garden earlier."

Ella looked worried. "I told her not to. I was scared she'd get lost in the snow again. I suppose it was silly to think she wouldn't go out."

"I don't think you need to worry, Ella," her mum said reassuringly. "Fluff's not a baby any more. I know she's still tiny, but she *has* grown! She's definitely old enough to be out there."

"But it's been snowing really hard today, Mum! And Fluff *always* comes back to see me when I get home from school. Always." Ella got up to peer out of the kitchen window. "The snow's really deep in the garden. She could easily have got confused about where she was going. Oh, why didn't I just lock the cat flap?"

"Ella, it's not fair to lock it, unless we really need to. Fluff wouldn't understand why she couldn't go out. She'd just get upset." But Ella's mum came to join her at the window. "You're right though, it *is* odd that she isn't back yet. I wonder where she's got to."

"We should go out and look for her," Ella said, heading for the hallway to put all her outdoor things back on.

"Oh, Ella, no, I'm sure we don't need to. Sit down, finish your hot chocolate. Honestly, Fluff was having a lovely time out there earlier on. She was playing with the snowflakes. She's probably just got too caught up with exploring. I'm sure she'll be home in a minute."

Ella trailed reluctantly back to the table. She knew Mum was right, but something was still niggling at her. Fluff had *never* missed meeting her before.

Ella's mum didn't sit back down, but stayed thoughtfully staring out of the window. She wished she was as sure as she was making out to Ella. She didn't think Fluff was lost, but she *was* worried. Fluff should have been back – was she hiding out somewhere, waiting for the snow to stop? She just couldn't help feeling that it was an awfully cold day for a small kitten to be stuck outside...

Fluff stood up, her whiskers twitching. Usually hearing another cat would have made her fur stand on end, and she'd be wanting to fight and defend her territory. But there was something about that cry. She didn't think that the cat making that noise was going to be putting up much of a fight. She picked her way out of her blanket nest, and stood still, listening carefully. She'd been so sleepy when she heard the mewing that she wasn't quite sure where it had come from.

There it was again. So quiet. So weak. Fluff listened anxiously. The other cat wasn't in this room, she was almost sure. She picked her way over the rubbish and fallen bricks, and peered through the doorway.

The cottage was tiny, only two rooms. The inner room was full of broken furniture, and Fluff leaped up on to an old chair to try and see what was happening. The room was silent, and she looked around worriedly. She was sure she hadn't imagined it. Although – the mew had seemed to be part of her dream at first... No! There it was again. The cry was coming from a battered cupboard on the other side of the room. Fluff wove her way carefully through the junk, and nosed at the door.

It swung open slightly, and cautiously she stuck her head inside.

Staring back at her out of the gloom was an enormous pair of green eyes.

The mew came again, and Fluff watched in horror as a tiny white kitten struggled to its feet, desperately trying to reach her.

The kitten could hardly stand, and at once Fluff jumped into the cupboard, nosing the little creature gently. She towered over it. This kitten was far too young to be on her own! She looked as though she was only just old enough to eat food, rather than milk from her mother. Where *was* her mother? Fluff could smell that at least one other cat had been here. Maybe this was where the kitten had been born. Cats often chose odd places to have their kittens – *she* had been born in a stable, and the horse it belonged to hadn't been happy at all.

But the mother cat's scent was fading. This kitten had been alone for a while, Fluff thought. She had to be starving. She was nuzzling hopefully at

Fluff, as though she thought Fluff might have brought her some food, but eventually she gave up, and collapsed down again. The cupboard was lined with rags, like the nest Fluff had made, and the white kitten lay down, curling herself up tight. She looked cold. Fluff lay down gently, curling herself around the kitten, like her own mother used to snuggle up to Fluff and her brothers and sisters.

The kitten mewed again, an even smaller sound this time, but she sounded pleased. Fluff purred comfortingly. Go to sleep. Maybe we can find your mother, she thought. But she had a horrible feeling that the kitten's mother was far away. Somehow they'd been separated.

Fluff rested her head gently next to the little white ears, watching anxiously as the kitten twitched her way to sleep. Fluff's tummy rumbled, but at least she'd had breakfast, which was more than she guessed the kitten had. She could feel the tiny body warming up, and her own eyes began to close.

Curled around each other, the two cats slept, alone in the snowy night.

Chapter Five

Ella got up at six the next morning. It was still practically dark, but she didn't care. She felt as though she hadn't slept at all, though she supposed she must have done. All her plans for a weekend of fun in the snow had gone – Fluff still wasn't back. Ella went downstairs, put on her winter coat, hat and scarf, and unlocked the back door.

The cat flap swung open as she went out, and she felt like kicking it. She *should* have locked it, no matter what Mum said. She would rather have a grumpy Fluff than no Fluff at all.

Out in the back garden the snow looked even deeper. There must have been another big fall in the night. Ella shivered. It was really freezing, even wrapped up as she was. She sighed. The garden looked so beautiful, all white with patches of green and icicles hanging from the branches. It was like a Christmas card – there was even a robin perched on the fence, looking at her hopefully to see if she was about to put crumbs out. Ella smiled a very small smile. If Fluff had been here, she would have been jumping up and down under the fence trying to get him. But all that proved was that Fluff definitely *wasn't* anywhere in the garden. Tucking her hands under her arms to try and keep them warm, Ella walked down the path – or rather, where she thought the path ought to be, as she couldn't see it at all.

"Fluff! Fluff, come on. Breakfast!" she called, trying to sound cheerful.

She stared round the garden, willing a stripy little furry body to come shooting out of the bushes. Then her heart leaped as she saw something moving at the bottom of the garden. "Fluff!" she squeaked delightedly, running towards her. "Oh, Fluff, you had me so worried. You bad cat, I thought I'd lost you again. Oh!" Ella stopped still as the strange cat stared up at her in surprise. It looked rather offended – as though it had been minding its own business, going for a morning walk, and suddenly it was being chased by a screaming girl. It twitched its tail irritably, and strolled on over the snow in a very dignified and haughty way, deliberately ignoring Ella.

"Sorry…" Ella whispered after it. She knew it was stupid to apologize to a cat, but it seemed to be the kind of cat who would expect her to. Now she could see it properly, it didn't even look much like Fluff. It was loads bigger, and its tabby coat was more spotted than striped. Trying not to cry, she plodded back to the house.

Her parents were in the kitchen making breakfast. They were both dressed, which wasn't normal for a Saturday. Usually everyone got up slowly, enjoying the weekend.

"Any luck?" Ella's dad asked. "We heard you calling."

Ella shook her head.

"I thought I saw her," she said miserably. "But it was another cat."

"I'm sure she's just waiting for the snow to stop," Ella's mum said briskly. "She'll be back soon. Sit down and have some breakfast, Ella."

"The snow *has* stopped," Ella pointed out, as she perched on the very edge of a chair. "So why isn't she back?"

Ella's parents glanced at each other with raised eyebrows, and she glared at them. "You're not taking this seriously!" she burst out. "Fluff's lost, I'm sure she is. We have to go and look for her."

Her dad sighed. "I have to say, I'm surprised she isn't back. She's never stayed out this long before, has she?"

Ella's mum nodded reluctantly. "I suppose not. I've just been hoping she'd pop through the cat flap any minute, but maybe we should go and look for her.

We should probably start by asking the neighbours if they've seen her."

Ella leaped up from the chair, heading for the door.

"Ella!" her mum yelled after her. "It's half-past six! On a Saturday! You cannot go and wake up the whole street. Eat some breakfast first."

A couple of hours later, Ella and her parents had asked up and down the street, but no one had seen Fluff. Everyone was upset to hear she was missing – lots of the neighbours had said how sweet she was, and how she often came up to be stroked and fussed over. Ella's parents had asked people to keep an eye out, and check that she wasn't shut in any garages or sheds.

"Mrs Jones's curtains are open now," Ella pointed out, as they trudged back up the street. "Can we go and ask her? Fluff loves her garden, she spends ages watching her fish in the pond."

"We might as well," her mum agreed.

Mrs Jones was horrified. "Poor thing," she said, sounding really worried. "It's so cold out. Oh, Ella, I'm sorry," she added, seeing Ella's eyes fill with tears. "You must be beside yourself, especially with her being lost before. I'm sure she'll turn up. She's such a bright little thing. She's probably just found herself a nice warm spot to see the snow out."

"Have you been out in your garden?" Ella said, sniffing. "She might be by your pond."

"The pond's frozen," Mrs Jones replied. "I saw her looking at it yesterday, she seemed very confused." She shook her head. "I don't think she's out there now, Ella, but you're welcome to go and check." She held the door open. "Why don't you all come and have a cup of tea, you must be freezing."

She led the way into the kitchen, and unlocked her garden door for Ella to go out. Ella's parents sat down gratefully. They were just sipping the tea, when Ella dashed back in, tears streaming down her face.

"Ella! What is it?" her mum asked, leaping up. "What's happened? Is Fluff—?"

Gulping, Ella stretched out her hand, and laid something small and wet on the table next to the teacups.

It was Fluff's collar.

Fluff woke up as a cold draught cut through the door to the cupboard, and made her flicker her ears uneasily. It took a few moments for her to work out where she was, then she looked down worriedly at the white kitten. She was curled into a tiny ball, right up against Fluff's tummy, and she was deeply asleep. Fluff licked her gently, and she laid her ears back, but didn't wake up. Fluff knew that she had to try and find her way home. Ella would be desperate, and the longer she left it, the harder it would be to find any tracks to help her get back. And she was starving! She'd missed her tea, and breakfast. That made her feel guilty, though – who knew when the younger kitten had last had anything to eat? Fluff eyed her thoughtfully. She hadn't sounded hungry last night. Was she so weak that she'd forgotten to be hungry? That was bad, very bad. Fluff needed to get home at once, and the little one had to wake up and come too. Fluff nosed her firmly, and she gave a faint, complaining mew, then opened her green eyes and stared accusingly at Fluff.

Fluff licked her again, apologetically, then butted her in the chest to make her stand up. The kitten mewed miserably, and tottered to her feet. Fluff stared at her, suddenly realizing that even now she was warmed up, this tiny creature was not going anywhere.

Fluff had found it almost impossible to stagger through the snow the day before – and this kitten was very weak!

But what should Fluff do? She didn't want to leave the kitten behind, either. Helplessly, she watched as the little white cat gave another feeble mew and slumped back down again. No, she certainly wasn't coming on an expedition through the snow. Fluff would just have to go and find Ella, and bring her back to help. The wailing wind had died down now, leaving an eerie silence, and Fluff thought the snow must have stopped. She would be able to see where she was heading. She felt better now she had made a decision, and she nosed her way out of the cupboard, and across the room.

She wanted to find some of the rags of blanket she had curled up in yesterday. The kitten wasn't so frozen now, but without Fluff to keep her warm, she would quickly get cold again. Dragging the blanket back with her teeth, she wrapped it round the kitten.

A tiny purr rumbled through the scrap of white fur, making Fluff feel even more determined. She had to find help. Giving the kitten one last worried glance, she pushed the cupboard door to with her nose to keep the cold out, and set off.

Fluff peered cautiously out of the hole in the cottage door, and shivered. The snow was even deeper now, but at least it seemed to have frozen hard. She stepped out, and looked helplessly around. Which way should she go? She had no idea. Even if she'd been able to remember which way she'd come, it all looked different now. Even the smells were covered in snow. She took a few uncertain steps, hoping to recognize something soon.

Then, to her horror, Fluff noticed snowflakes spiralling down. More snow! She looked up, hoping it would be just a light shower, but the sky was full of them, falling thickly down towards her. She needed to get back under cover fast – she knew from yesterday that there was no point trying to go anywhere in this. But perhaps she had time to find some food, before the storm got too heavy? Fluff looked around hopefully, but only saw trees. No good.

Hurrying back into the cottage, she noticed something she'd not seen in the dark the evening before. A battered old bag, lying by the door. Eagerly, Fluff clawed at it, retrieving a foil-wrapped packet. Ham sandwiches!

They didn't smell very fresh, but she was in no position to be fussy, and neither was the kitten.

The kitten did *not* want to be woken again. Fluff had to cuff her nose to make her sit up and take notice of the food. She sniffed at it reluctantly, too tired to bother, but Fluff knew the kitten had to eat. She bit off a tiny piece of ham, and then nudged it against the kitten's mouth until she opened it to protest. As the taste of the food hit her tongue, she brightened a little, swallowing it down, and looked hopefully at Fluff for more. Fluff bit off some more pieces, gulping a few down herself. The kitten managed several mouthfuls, then curled up to sleep again.

Fluff watched her, feeling relieved. Surely the food would help her? She devoured the rest of the sandwich, then tucked herself back round the kitten. There didn't seem to be much else to do but sleep, so she slept.

It was much, much colder when she woke again. She was shivering, even wrapped up in their blanket nest. The kitten wasn't. She was completely still, and for an awful moment Fluff thought she wasn't even breathing.

There was a tiny snuffle of breath, but it was so shallow – as though the kitten could hardly be bothered. When Fluff tried to rouse her, she wouldn't wake. She was too cold.

Fluff stood up. The cold seemed to be inside her now, a freezing fear that she wouldn't be able to save this little one. The kitten had no one to help her but Fluff. Even if it was still snowing, she had to go, *now*, and find Ella, and bring her back.

Chapter Six

Fluff staggered through the snow, her paws aching with the cold. Every so often she had to stop and rest, taking in deep shaking breaths of the burning cold air, and each time it was harder to set off again. But she couldn't give up. She was desperate to find Ella now. If Fluff could just keep going, surely she would find her soon, and she'd be home and in the warm, and Ella would be able to help the snow-white kitten. She ploughed on, trying not to think of the cold, just imagining the big bowl of tuna fish that Ella would give her...

"Ella, sweetheart, we have to go back home now. It's turned really cold – it's not good for us to be out in this for so long." Ella's mum was looking really anxious.

"But Mum, Fluff's out in it!" Ella cried. "And she's tiny and she isn't wearing a great big coat and boots and a hat and—"

"Yes, yes, I know." Mum sighed. "Just a little longer then. We've been up and down the street twice now though, I don't know where else to look."

"What about that little wood that backs on to the gardens further down?" Ella's dad suggested.

"Well, yes, I suppose she could have got in there," Mum agreed doubtfully. "It's worth a try."

"There's an alleyway round the corner, we can get in that way." Dad strode off, Ella trotting beside him.

They were a few steps in among the trees when Mum held Ella back. "I'm not sure this is a good idea after all," she told Ella. "The snow must have blown right in here, it's really deep, and there's bound to be tree roots and things hidden under the snowdrifts. You could break an ankle."

"Mmmm." Ella's dad looked thoughtful. "You're right. Maybe we should poke a branch into the snow to make sure we aren't about to fall into anything dangerous."

Ella wasn't listening. Letting go of her dad's arm, she took a shaky step forward, and crouched down. Her parents watched in amazement as a tiny grey shape staggered towards them through the gloomy, snow-filled wood. Ella was crying, tears tracking down her face without her even noticing.

Fluff put on a burst of speed and shot into Ella's arms, curling her head joyfully in under Ella's chin, and purring with relief and happiness. She'd found Ella. She was back. She was safe.

For a few moments she allowed herself to enjoy being stroked and cuddled and told how brave she was, and how naughty to go running off in the snow. Then she wriggled herself out from Ella's tight embrace, putting her paws against Ella's chest and mewing urgently.

"What's the matter?" Ella looked confused. Fluff had seemed so happy to see them, but now it was obvious that she wanted something.

Fluff struggled out of Ella's arms and jumped lightly down, looking back up at Ella, and mewing again. *Follow me!* she was saying, as clearly as she could. She trotted a few paces back into the wood, and looked round at Ella beseechingly.

"What's she doing?" Dad asked. "Fluff, that's not the way home. Come on!"

"She wants us to follow her," Ella said firmly. "Look, she's calling us." And she set off after Fluff, who bounded ahead delightedly, all her tiredness gone. Only a few moments before, she had felt as though she was going to drop down in the snow and sleep. She had been struggling through the drifts for over an hour, trying to find any signs of the way home. But now she was back with Ella, she had a surge of new energy.

"Ella, be careful!" her mum called. "Don't trip over any fallen branches!" Ella's parents scrambled after them. They had no idea where they were going, but it was clear that Fluff was trying to get them to follow, anyone could see that. Every so often she would turn round to check they were still with her, then head off again, following her paw prints purposefully back through the trees.

There it was! Fluff jumped through the door of the cottage, popping her head back out to call to Ella. Ella crouched down to squeeze through the gap in the door after her.

"Ella, no!" her mum yelled. "Be careful, you don't know what's in there!"

"It's OK, Mum," Ella called back. "I'm following Fluff, it's fine."

Her mother tried to catch her up and stop her, worried that the old building might be falling down, but she slipped on the snow, and slid over, falling on to her hands and knees just in time to see Ella disappearing into the building. Ella's dad stopped to help her up, and they skidded over to look through the window.

Fluff wove her way hurriedly through the cottage, still calling to Ella to follow.

"I'm coming, I'm coming, Fluff! I can't fit underneath all this stuff like you can!" Ella puffed, scrambling over a pile of old sofa cushions. "I wish I knew what you were trying to show me, anyway." She realized that Fluff had stopped next to an old cupboard that was jammed up against the far wall. She was peering round the door, her body tense, nervous, almost scared – as though she wasn't sure what she was going to find. Ella walked quietly up to Fluff, and knelt behind her, but she couldn't see what Fluff was looking at. Suddenly some of the stiffness went out of Fluff's spine, and she reached gently into the cupboard. She backed carefully

out, carrying something in her mouth –
something quite large. She dropped it in
Ella's lap, and it was only as Fluff sat
back and gazed hopefully up at her, that
Ella realized what it was. Fluff had just
given her a kitten! She had pulled it out
of the cupboard like a magic trick.

"Fluff! It's a kitten! Where did you—?"

Fluff mewed urgently at her, and Ella looked more closely. She stroked the tiny white head, and saw that the little creature didn't stir. She gave Fluff an anxious look, her heart thudding with nervousness. Fluff looked back up at her lovingly.

"I don't know," Ella said worriedly. "She's so little and weak, Fluff. I – I'm not even sure she's still breathing." She stood up, cradling the tiny furry ball gently. "Come on. We need to get her to a vet." Very carefully she wrapped the kitten in her scarf, and tucked the parcel inside her jacket. She wasn't sure she could clamber over all that junk carrying her.

Ella's parents were calling her as they headed back, and her dad was starting to pull away the boards blocking the door.

"Ella! There you are!" he said angrily as she crouched to go through the hole. "What have you been doing? You should never have gone in there; what have we told you about playing in dangerous places like that?"

"I wasn't playing, Dad!" Ella said indignantly. "Look!" And she opened her jacket to show them her tiny passenger. "Fluff found her. But I'm not sure—" Her voice wobbled. "I can't see her breathing," she whispered, tears stinging the corners of her eyes.

"Let me see." Her dad lifted the kitten out, and she lay floppy and lifeless in his big hands. He was silent for a horribly long moment. "She is. But only just. Come on, we need to get home right now and ring the vet. We need to tell them we've got an emergency coming in."

Ella had been to the vet's surgery before, to take Fluff to have all her vaccinations, but this time there was no hanging around in the reception. She and her parents raced in, Ella cradling the kitten, and were rushed straight through to the surgery. It was the same vet who'd looked after Fluff before, and she smiled, recognizing Ella.

"The receptionist said you'd found a stray kitten?" she asked, gently taking the scarf-wrapped bundle from Ella.

Ella nodded. "She's so tiny, and she's only just breathing," she explained. "It wasn't really us that found her though, it was Fluff."

"We think she must have been

abandoned by her mother," Ella's dad put in. "Fluff and Ella found her in an old cottage on some woodland near us."

The vet nodded thoughtfully. "She looks about three or four weeks old to me. Only just old enough to survive without her mother. She's very weak – I think she's had a couple of days on her own in the cold. I'm going to put her on a drip to get some food into her, and we'll put her in an incubator, get her really nice and warm." She smiled, looking at Ella's anxious face. "I think you found her just in time. I can't promise, but it looks to me as if she's just cold and hungry, nothing worse. You might even be able to take her home in a couple of hours." She started to get the equipment she needed.

"Oh, that's fantastic!" Ella squeaked, not noticing that Mum and Dad looked a bit shocked. "That's really good, because I don't think Fluff will understand where she is. She looked so upset when we drove off. She was watching us through the window—"

"Ella, Ella, hang on," Mum interrupted. "We don't know who this kitten belongs to. And we already have Fluff, I'm not sure we can—"

"Mum!" Ella was horrified. "We have to take her home! Fluff saved her – what are you going to tell Fluff if we go back without her?"

Dad looked thoughtful. "Didn't the people who moved from that house down the road a few days ago have a white cat? I'm sure I remember seeing one around. Was she pregnant? Maybe she decided to have her kittens in that cottage. Cats do that sometimes, don't they?" he asked the vet. "Find strange places to have their kittens?"

The vet nodded. "It's to do with wanting to be private, and keeping the kittens safe. If her owners were moving, she might not have liked all the mess of packing up at home." She was laying the white kitten in what looked like a fish tank. "This has got a heat mat to warm her up gently," she explained. "I'll take her through to the ward when she's settled."

Ella peered through the plastic side. The kitten looked really cosy, but that gave her a horrible thought. "What happened to the other kittens?" she asked worriedly. "Do you think they're outside somewhere? There was only this little one in the cupboard."

"Maybe the mother carried them back to the house," the vet said thoughtfully. "Or perhaps she only had the one. That happens sometimes, and it would mean that it wasn't too obvious she was going to have kittens. Her owners might not have known."

Mum looked sad. "So they took her with them and left the kitten behind."

"Yes, she might have had to go home for some food. Thank goodness for Fluff," the vet said, smiling.

Mum sighed, and shook her head. "I suppose you're right, Ella. After what Fluff did, we have to take this one home too." Then she smiled. "I might have known it wouldn't stop with one!"

"You mean we can keep her?" Ella asked, hopping up and down. "Really?"

Her dad grinned. "Why not. I took ages putting in that cat flap, we might as well use it… Ooof!" he gasped as Ella hurled herself at him for a hug.

"Thank you, thank you, thank you! I can't wait to tell Fluff!"

Back at home Fluff was sitting anxiously on the window sill. She didn't quite understand where Ella and the kitten had gone, but Ella had whispered that they were looking after her. She stared out at the snowy street, watching for the car, waiting for Ella. As they pulled up in front of the house, she jumped up with her paws scrabbling on the glass, mewing excitedly. Where was the kitten?

Ella got carefully out of the car, and Fluff watched in relief as she walked slowly up the path, cradling the kitten. Fluff was there waiting as they opened the door, twining affectionately around Ella's ankles, then leading Ella to the kitchen and her too-big basket. She watched as Ella carefully set the kitten down on the red cushion, then she stepped in and curled herself around the white kitten lovingly. The kitten, who'd been fast asleep ever since they left the vet's, opened one eye sleepily, and looked up at Fluff. "Prrrp," she murmured, and a very small bright-pink tongue shot out and licked Fluff's nose. Then she went back to sleep.

Fluff looked down at her, and then back at Ella, who was crouched next to the basket watching.

Ella reached over to scratch Fluff under the chin. "What shall we call her?" she wondered, looking at the kitten's white fur, snuggled next to Fluff's tabby coat. "How about Snowy?

She *is* our snow rescue kitten."

Fluff yawned and stretched a little in agreement.

Ella grinned, watching the two of them snooze. "It looks like we were right to buy a big basket after all!"

Look out for:

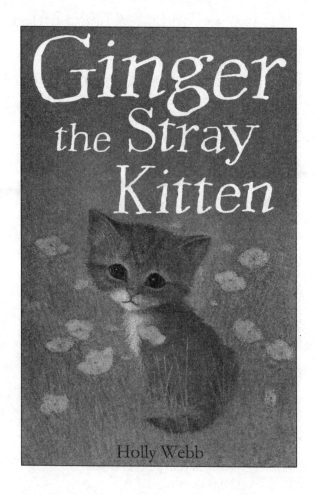

Ginger
the Stray
Kitten

Holly Webb

Also available:

Sky the Unwanted Kitten

Holly Webb

From the author of LOST IN THE SNOW

Max the
Missing
Puppy

Holly Webb

From the author of LOST IN THE SNOW

Sam the Stolen Puppy

Holly Webb

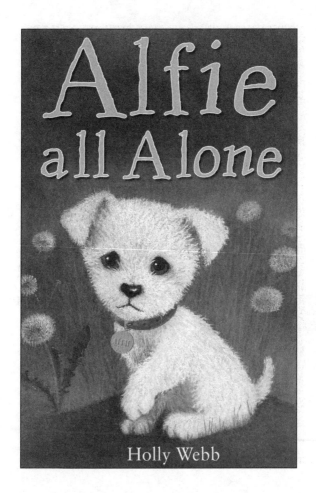

Alfie
all Alone

Holly Webb

Animal Rescue
Tina Nolan

Abandoned ... lost ... neglected?
There's always a home at Animal Magic!

In a perfect world there'd be no need
for Animal Magic. But Eva and Karl
Harrison, who live at the animal rescue
centre with their parents, know that life
isn't perfect. Every day there's a new
arrival in need of their help!

Honey
The unwanted puppy

Charlie
The home-alone kitten

Merlin
The homeless foal

Rusty
The injured fox cub

Bella
The runaway rabbit

Dilly
The lost duckling

Harry
The abandoned hamster

Barney
The baby hedgehog

Holly
The doorstep puppy

Rosie
The problem pony

Pony Camp Diaries

By Kelly McKain

Saddle up for a week in pony paradise!

Welcome to Sunnyside Stables, and
the pony holiday of your dreams!
Written in diary form, each book follows
a different girl's adventures at Pony
Camp, as she gets her very own pony,
makes new friends and tackles tough
new challenges!

Megan and *Mischief*
Kelly McKain

Poppy and *Prince*
Kelly McKain

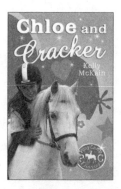

Chloe and *Cracker*
Kelly McKain

Sophie and *Shine*
Kelly McKain

Charlie and *Charm*
Kelly McKain

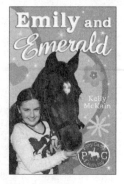

Emily and *Emerald*
Kelly McKain

Dirty Bertie

David Roberts
Written by Alan MacDonald

Meet Dirty Bertie – the boy with nose-pickingly DISGUSTING habits!

These fantastic 3-in-1 storybooks featuring the world's grubbiest trouble magnet are guaranteed to have you in stitches. So if it's comic chaos you're after then look no further – Bertie is sure to be up to his neck in it!

BEWARE!
BERTIE'S REVOLTING HABITS COULD RUB OFF ON YOU!

Also available:

The Fairies of Starshine Meadow

Kate Bloom
Illustrated by Emma Pack

Wishes big and wishes small,
With my wand I'll grant them all!

Meet four fairy friends from Starshine
Meadow – Belle, Daisy, Ivy and Rose.
With the help of the Dandelion Queen,
they love to make dreams come true!

The Fairies of
Starshine Meadow

Making wishes come true!

Ivy and the
Fantastic Friend

Kate Bloom and Emma Pack

The Fairies of
Starshine Meadow

Making wishes come true!

Belle and the
Magic Makeover

Kate Bloom and Emma Pack

The Fairies of
Starshine Meadow

Making wishes come true!

Daisy and the
Dazzling Drama

Kate Bloom and Emma Pack

The Fairies of
Starshine Meadow

Making wishes come true!

Rose and the
Perfect Pet

Kate Bloom and Emma Pack

Lost in the Storm

Now flip me over to read

Lost in the Snow

Holly Webb

Illustrated by Sophy Williams

For Sammy and Marble,
and for the original Rosie

STRIPES PUBLISHING
An imprint of Magi Publications
1 The Coda Centre, 189 Munster Road,
London SW6 6AW

A paperback original
This edition exclusive to Waterstone's 2008

Lost in the Snow first published in Great Britain in 2006
Lost in the Storm first published in Great Britain in 2007

Text copyright © Holly Webb, 2006, 2007
Illustrations copyright © Sophy Williams, 2006, 2007

ISBN: 978-1-84715-089-9

A CIP catalogue record for this book is available
from the British Library.

Printed and bound in Germany.

10 9 8 7 6 5 4 3 2 1

Chapter One

Rosebridge Farm was a beautiful place in the autumn. The leaves on the big oak tree at the corner of the farmyard had turned golden, and every so often a few of them would whirl down to the ground and give the hens a fright. The farm was a lovely old place, and the Moffat family had been dairy farmers there for over a hundred years.

There were stables, and a big barn, and a beautiful old farmhouse that looked cosy and inviting in the autumn sunshine.

But today no one at the farm was noticing how lovely it all was. Mrs Moffat and her son Ben were in the office, looking at the accounts, and worrying. It had been a difficult year, and money was tight. Outside in the yard, Sara, Mrs Moffat's thirteen-year-old daughter, was trying to give the hen house a makeover. "Ow!" she yelped, as she hit herself with the hammer for the fourth time. "Sorry, chicks," she said to the hens, who were scratching and pecking round her feet. "You're just going to have to wait for Ben to come and help me." She put down the

hammer and headed off to the farmhouse, but as she passed the stables something made her stop.

What was that funny squeaking noise? Sara peered over the half-door at Gus, their old pony. He gazed back, and snorted, shaking himself all over. Then he nosed down at a pile of straw practically underneath him. His face seemed to be saying that he wasn't complaining, but really, of all the places…

"Rosie! You've had the kittens!" exclaimed Sara excitedly. She leaned so far over the door she nearly fell into the stable. Rosie the farm cat glared at her. "Sorry, sorry! I promise I won't come in and disturb you. I just want to have a quick look."

The kittens were snuggled up next to Rosie in Gus's bed of straw. They were tripping over each other, as they nuzzled gently at their mother, still blind and helpless.

"Oh, they're gorgeous, Rosie! So how many are there? Two black ones, a ginger – oh no, two gingers. I wish you'd hold still, kittens, I'm counting. And a tabby – oh. Oh dear." Sara's delighted voice flattened. The tabby kitten was so tiny – much, much smaller than her brothers and sisters – and she was hardly moving.

"Oh, I do hope you'll be all right!" Sara whispered worriedly, as one of the others climbed over it. But she had a horrible feeling that the tiny thing was just too small to survive…

Even though Sara had lived on the farm all her life, and she knew that this sort of thing just happened sometimes, her eyes filled with tears.

The littlest kitten was so sweet – it had really long fur and looked like a little bundle of fluff! As she watched, it got trodden on again, and opened its mouth in a tiny, almost silent mew of protest. Sara wiped her sleeve across her eyes sadly.

She took one last look at the kittens – at least the other four looked fit and healthy – and dashed off to tell her mum and Ben.

"Rosie's had her kittens!" she called, as she opened the kitchen door.

10

Mrs Moffat popped her head round the door of the office. "Oh lovely! How many are there?"

"Five, but—"

"Five more mouths to feed," a gloomy voice sighed. Ben was at agricultural college, training in farm management. He loved Rosebridge Farm, all the Moffats did, but he hated it that things weren't going well. The farm was hardly making enough money to live on at the moment, and Ben was counting every penny.

"Oh, they're only tiny mouths, Ben! We can feed five little kittens!" laughed his mother.

"I think it might only be four soon," said Sara. "The little tabby one – it's so small. I'm not sure it'll make it."

"Oh dear," said Mrs Moffat, jumping up and coming out to the kitchen. "Let's take a look, Sara, where are they?"

Sara led her mum and Ben out to see the new family, hoping that her mum would say she was making a fuss about nothing. But Mrs Moffat looked at the littlest kitten sadly. "I think you might be right, Sara. It's too little. What a pity."

"Please don't call her an it, Mum, I'm sure she's a little girl kitten."

"I know what you mean, she's so pretty and delicate, with those lovely brown and black markings." Mrs Moffat sighed.

"Isn't there anything we can do?" Sara asked, tears filling her eyes again.

"Well, I suppose we could try her with some of that special kitten milk out of an eye-dropper," her mum said doubtfully. "That's if Rosie will let us. But Sara, listen, you mustn't let yourself get too attached to her. I'm really sorry, but her chances just aren't good."

Over the next couple of weeks, Sara wondered if Rosie had heard them saying that the tabby kitten wasn't likely to survive. Rosie was a stubborn old cat, and she seemed determined to prove everyone wrong. She always made sure that the tabby kitten got an extra turn suckling, and by the time the kittens were three weeks old and

starting to explore the stable, the littlest kitten was still little, but she was catching up. Rosie was very protective of them, but she did let Sara and her mum in to feed the tabby, and cuddle them all every so often. The littlest kitten fought for more than her fair share of cuddles, and would lie in Sara's arms, purring a purr that seemed far too loud for such a tiny creature.

It wasn't long before the bigger kittens got bored with exploring the stable and playing tag round Gus's hooves, and started trying to escape outside.

One morning the two ginger boy kittens hid behind the stable door. As soon as Sara opened it, they shot out into the farmyard. They seemed a bit

surprised by how much world there was out there, but they certainly weren't going back in. Rosie seemed to realize that she couldn't keep them all shut up any longer, so she shooed the other kittens out too. But the tabby cried, and hid behind Rosie – outside was just too big and scary.

Rosie nudged the little kitten to the door, where she mewed miserably, her tiny paws scrabbling as she fought to get back into the safety of the cosy stable.

"Rosie, don't be such a bully!" said Sara, scooping up the trembling kitten. "Poor little ball of fluff, she's scared."

The kitten snuggled into Sara's fleece – this was a much better place to be. And she'd heard that word "fluff"

again. Everyone seemed to say it when they saw her. *Perhaps Fluff is my name?* she thought happily.

Sara, Ben and Mrs Moffat had decided not to give any of the kittens names, as they knew that they wouldn't be at the farm for very long. As soon as the kittens were eight weeks old, they'd be old enough to leave Rosie, and find new homes.

But it was hard not to call the little one Fluff. Sara gave in first, and Ben and her mum told her off about it.

"I told you not to get attached to any of them!" her mum scolded. "If you give her a name you'll want her to stay, and you know we can't afford it."

"Eating us out of house and home as it is," muttered Ben, stroking the little kitten under the chin, and trying not to grin as her massive purr rumbled round the stable.

"But she just is a Fluff!" cried Sara, grinning. "Look at her, she's the world's fluffiest kitten!"

It was true. And Fluff had beautiful markings too; a fluffy brown and black tabby coat, huge white paws, and a white shirt-front. She'd inherited Rosie's dark brown eyes, and although she had a huge purr, her mew was still the same tiny little noise that had broken Sara's heart the day she'd been born.

It seemed no time at all before the kittens were eight weeks old. Fluff was still small compared to the others, and she looked even smaller because she

seemed to be all fluff, whereas her brothers and sisters had short silky-smooth coats. Sara watched them as they played in the yard. The two black girl kittens were exploring an old bucket, while the two ginger boys played tug of war with a piece of string. As usual, Fluff was sat on her own watching her brothers and sisters, too timid to join in. Sara sighed … she couldn't help feeling sorry for the little kitten, she always seemed to be left out of their fun and games.

Mrs Moffat and Ben appeared at the back door with steaming mugs of tea. "I know you'd like to keep them all, Sara, but I think the kittens are big enough to leave Rosie now," said Mrs Moffat, as she watched them playing.

"I'll put a sign up on the gate, saying they're free to good homes. I can put up the signs for Christmas wreaths at the same time – making those always brings in extra money at this time of year. And we need every penny," she smiled.

Sara and Ben made faces. The farm was on the outskirts of Fairford, and lots of people came to buy holly wreaths and mistletoe at Christmas. The wreaths made a lot of money, but it meant spending December with prickled fingers.

"It's a pity," Ben said, watching Fluff half-heartedly chase a piece of string. "I shouldn't think anyone will want the little fluffy one – she's so skinny, she looks half-starved."

"How can you be so cruel, she's gorgeous!" Sara protested. But secretly, she couldn't help hoping Ben was right. Fluff was her favourite and she couldn't imagine her out there in the big wide world beyond the farm.

Chapter Two

Fluff and the other kittens knew that they would all be leaving to go to new homes soon. Whenever there were visitors they had to be on their best behaviour in the hope that someone might want to take them home. It had been the same with Rosie's last litter of kittens.

Fluff wasn't sure about it all. She

loved Rosebridge Farm. But then a home of her own did sound wonderful. Fluff's brothers and sisters were very excited, and kept trying to sneak out when the gates were open.

Every time there was a customer for the lovely Christmas wreaths, Mrs Moffat would point out the kittens, frisking prettily in the yard. It wasn't long before the two black girl kittens were snapped up by a lady who fell in love with them as they wove themselves round her legs.

It looked so easy, Fluff thought, and the next day she waited for a friendly-looking customer and tried it for herself. But she tripped the man up, and he stomped off with wet and muddy trousers.

25

The ginger kittens found owners a few days later, and Fluff watched them being carried away in a beautiful basket. She felt very alone. Rosie was still there, and Gus, and the hens, but it wasn't the same without her brothers and sisters. Even though they'd laughed at her, Fluff missed them. She took to sitting on top of Gus's half-door, and moping.

Rosie tried to persuade her back down, but Fluff preferred to stay where she was. Rosie gave up eventually, but when they curled up in the hay to sleep that night, she was extra-affectionate to Fluff, nuzzling her comfortingly. The big tabby cat wrapped her tail round her last little kitten, and purred as she drifted off to sleep.

But Fluff lay awake, fretting. She knew that her mother was disappointed to have such a skinny, nervous kitten. What was going to happen to her? Mrs Moffat kept looking at her worriedly, and Fluff couldn't help thinking, *What happens to kittens that nobody wants?*

A few days later, Fluff was perched up on Gus's door when a car drew up outside the farmyard. Fluff had given up trying to look lovable, as no one seemed to be interested in taking her home, so she stayed put and just watched.

A lady and her daughter had come to buy a holly wreath. The girl, who was about seven, ran round excitedly, desperate to explore. She poked her head into the hen house, and climbed the fence to look at the cows. Then she began exploring the yard. Her mum kept calling her back – "Ella! Don't get in the way! Ella! Don't get your shoes muddy!" – but Ella wasn't listening.

Then she saw Fluff.

"Oh, what a pretty kitten! Please can I stroke you? Puss?"

A pretty kitten? Does she mean me? Fluff was so surprised that she turned round to see if there was another kitten behind her, forgetting how carefully she was balanced on top of the door... She mewed frantically and clawed her way back up again.

"I'm sorry, I didn't mean to scare you, poor little bundle of fluff..."

Fluff looked at Ella in amazement. This girl knew her name! She reached out to the girl's hand and butted against it with her head, purring delightedly.

"Oh, aren't you sweet? Can I pick you up?" Ella asked, gently.

30

She certainly could! Fluff snuggled into her neck and licked her chin, making Ella giggle. She tickled Fluff's bright white shirt-front. "The sign outside said they needed homes for kittens. Maybe I could take you home? Mum and Dad promised I could have a pet soon, and you would be perfect."

Fluff purred blissfully. Someone wanted to take her home! Someone who was very, very good at stroking.

Please take me home! she mewed.

Ella carried Fluff back over to her mother, who was paying Mrs Moffat for the wreath.

"Oh, your little girl's found Fluff," said Mrs Moffat hopefully. "We're looking for a home for her, I don't suppose you—"

"Ella! Put that grubby little kitten down!" said Ella's mother in horror.

Grubby? Fluff laid her ears back. She wasn't grubby, was she? She opened her eyes wide at Ella's mother, and tried to look clean.

"Mum, she's not grubby, she's beautiful! Can't we take her home, please? She needs a home, and you did say I could have a pet soon."

"Yes, I know, but not a cat, Ella! A goldfish, maybe. Something nice and clean. And quiet."

"But I don't want a fish! I don't like fish, they're boring. You know I love cats, and Fluff's perfect. Please? I'll look after her."

"No, Ella, I'm sorry, but we don't want a cat in the house. Now come on,

we've got Christmas shopping to do."

"Mum, please!" Ella begged.

"No! Now put her down."

Ella's eyes filled with tears, but she put Fluff down gently, kissing the top of her head.

"I'm sorry, Fluff. I'd love to take you home, I think you're beautiful." Ella gave the little tabby one last stroke.

Fluff couldn't believe it. She watched Ella leave, confused, and mewing frantically. "Come back! Come back!" Someone had wanted her, wanted to give her a home. And now they were gone!

Chapter Three

That evening, Ella's mum was starting
to wish that she'd never taken Ella to
Rosebridge Farm. Ella had spent the
rest of the day talking non-stop about
Fluff, and when her dad arrived home
from work, she didn't even give him
the chance to take off his coat.

"Dad, you have to talk to Mum! You
did say I could have a pet, didn't you?

You promised! I've found the best pet ever, and Mum says I can't have her, and you have to help me persuade her!"

Ella's dad sighed. He had a feeling that this was one of those situations where he was going to get into trouble whatever he said. "Er, have you? That's nice," he murmured cautiously.

"No, it isn't! Because Mum says I can't have her, you have to talk to her!"

Ella grabbed his arm and dragged him into the kitchen.

Ella's mum was reading a magazine. She had been ignoring Ella entirely for the last hour, because however many times she explained that they couldn't have a cat, it didn't seem to be sinking in. She gave her husband a Look, which meant, "Don't you dare!"

Ella's dad plonked himself down at the table, and sighed. "Ella, I'm sorry, but I have no idea what you're talking about. Come and sit down and tell me again."

Ella huffed irritably, and grabbed the nearest chair. "You said I could have a pet. I've found the pet I want. So can I have her, please?" she said, in a pleading voice.

Ella's dad took a deep breath. "Ella, you know there's more to it than that. Mum and I did say you could have a pet, but it's got to be the right sort of pet."

"But this is the right sort of pet! She's beautiful!"

"Er, what is she exactly?"

"A cat, of course! The prettiest kitten ever, Dad! She's got gorgeous big eyes, and great fat paws, and the fluffiest fur you've ever seen. And she's so tiny, and she really needs a home. She's called Fluff. So can we go back to the farm and get her? Please?"

Ella's dad shook his head. "Ella, we said you could have a hamster! Maybe! If you were very good! Not a cat. We don't want a cat!"

Ella looked shocked. She'd been pinning all her hopes on her dad saying yes. "But why not?" she asked in a small voice. "She's such a sweet cat, Dad. You'd love her. Why don't you just come and see—"

"Ella, Dad said no!" her mum put in tiredly. "And I've already said no. You cannot have that cat, or any cat—"

"I don't want any cat! I want Fluff!" Ella said, her eyes tearing up.

She got up from the table and hurried up to her room. She couldn't believe that her parents had said no. Especially when poor Fluff needed a home so badly. What if no one ever came to take her home?

Chapter Four

The next morning, Fluff was still pining for Ella, in spite of Rosie's efforts to cheer her up.

She slunk out of the stable and batted a piece of paper sack backwards and forwards, occasionally summoning up the energy for a bit of a pounce, but it didn't stop her feeling miserable about Ella.

It wasn't long before a car pulled up in the road outside the farm, and a woman and her son appeared in the yard. Fluff didn't take much notice, until she heard the woman asking about kittens.

Mrs Moffat sounded delighted. "Actually, we've just the one left, but she's a dear little thing. She's there, look, playing with that bit of paper."

Mrs Moffat came over and picked Fluff up, stroking her gently and murmuring nice things. Fluff began to purr, even though she still felt sad. How lovely it would be to have someone to pet her like that all the time! These people couldn't be as nice as Ella, but at least they would give her a home. She rubbed a damp paw

quickly round her face, and tried to look clean.

"Isn't she cute?" said the woman, tickling Fluff under her chin. "She'll make you a lovely pet, won't she, Nathan?" she said to the boy.

Nathan didn't look convinced. He just glared at Fluff.

"You see, we want Nathan to have a pet to teach him a sense of responsibility," Nathan's mother said to Mrs Moffat. "He's been in a bit of trouble at school, and one of the teachers came up with the idea. A cat will be perfect."

Nathan spoke for the first time. "I don't want a cat. Cats are boring. Can't I have something cool, like a tarantula or a snake?"

"Don't be silly, Nathan," snapped his mother. "You know we all agreed on a cat."

Mrs Moffat began to look doubtful, and Fluff laid her ears back at the sound of the cross voices. She wasn't sure she liked this family after all.

"You know, I'm not sure… If your son doesn't really want Fluff, you might be better off—"

"Really, she'll be fine with us. Nathan will love her, once he gets used to the idea. Perhaps he could hold her?"

Mrs Moffat looked worriedly at Nathan's scowl, but his mother gave him a Look, and he seemed to remember his manners. "Please can I hold her?" he asked politely.

Still slightly unsure, Mrs Moffat handed him Fluff. Nathan held her as though he wasn't quite sure how to, and patted the top of her head. Too hard – Fluff felt grateful she had nice, thick fur to protect her.

"See, isn't she lovely? You'll be friends in no time." Nathan's mother turned to Mrs Moffat. "Could we take her now? I don't suppose you have a box or something that we could carry her home in?"

As soon as his mother and Mrs Moffat had gone to look for a box, Nathan stopped being quite so nice. He held Fluff out at arm's length and made a disgusted face at her.

"I'm not looking after you," he sneered. "Stupid, ratty little thing." He

grabbed the scruff of her neck, and poked her angrily. "I'll be stuck with feeding you and everything. Even a dog would be better." He made a growling noise. "Anyway, I won't have to bother for long. Next door's Alsatian will have you for breakfast."

Fluff looked at the boy with huge round eyes. This was not going to be a home, after all. If only she could just stay here! But Mrs Moffat had said all the kittens must go. She needed a proper home. Somewhere with a friendly, loving person to take care of her. She needed to find Ella!

Fluff's fur stood up on end. She hissed angrily at Nathan, then sank a mouthful of sharp little teeth into the finger that he was prodding her with. He yelped and dropped her. Fluff landed lightly on the floor and took a flying leap on to the farmyard wall. She was going to do what Rosie had always forbidden. She took a last look at her old home, and then she jumped down the other side of the wall. Mrs

Moffat and Nathan's mother came back into the yard just in time to see a fluffy tabby tail whisking over the wall, and Nathan looking shocked and guilty.

"Fluff!" Mrs Moffat cried, running to the gate. She wrenched it open and dashed outside. But there was no little kitten waiting to be called back in, no flash of tabby fur disappearing round the corner. Fluff was gone!

Chapter Five

On the other side of Fairford, Ella was lying on her bedroom floor drawing a picture. It was a picture she'd drawn at least twenty times already. Sometimes Fluff was sitting down, sometimes she was walking along the stable door, but she always looked sad. Sad and lonely, just like Ella was feeling. Ella fetched her best water-colouring pencils, and

started to colour in Fluff's lovely tabby fur, using a wet paintbrush to make it look soft and fluffy. How could her mum say Fluff was grubby? She was so beautiful! Ella carefully outlined Fluff's big eyes with black, and added her sparkling white whiskers and eyebrows. Then she got out her gel pens, and added a little silver tear trickling out of the corner of each eye.

"Ella, there you are." Ella hadn't even noticed her dad calling for her. It was Saturday, and he'd been out in the garden trimming the Christmas tree, preparing to bring it indoors. "That's beautiful. Is that Fluff?"

Ella nodded, and sniffed, and then a real tear splashed down on to the paper and made Fluff's fur run. It was ruined. Ella blinked back the tears, and sadly scrunched up the piece of paper. She'd given up arguing with her parents about Fluff, because it wasn't doing any good at all, but she couldn't stop being miserable, and worrying about the little kitten.

"Ella, will you come downstairs a minute. Your mum and I want to talk to you."

Ella sighed, but followed her dad downstairs. She knew what they were going to say. Mum and Dad were going to try to cheer her up again like they had earlier. So far, they'd suggested Christmas shopping, decorating the Christmas tree, and a trip to the pantomime. But even though the pantomime had been a fantastic treat, Ella just couldn't stop thinking about Fluff.

Her parents were sitting at the kitchen table, looking serious. Ella's mum took her hand. "Ella, your dad and I know you've been really sad about not being able to have Fluff. We've talked it over, and although we're still a bit worried about it, we've decided that you can have her after all—"

Ella didn't wait to hear more. She threw herself at her mum, knocking the breath out of her. "You mean it? Thank you, thank you, thank you!"

"Ella, listen. You can only have Fluff on the condition that you look after her properly. She'll need feeding twice a day, and grooming, especially if she's as fluffy as you say she is. You'll have to be very responsible." Dad's voice was serious, and Ella nodded.

"I'll look after her, I promise." Ella was beaming. She would do anything!

"Well, what are we waiting for?" Dad bounced up from the table. "Let's go and get her! Why don't we walk over to the farm? It's only a short walk to the other side of town, and it's a beautiful day."

Ella dashed into the hall and put on her pink sheepskin boots, and fluffy winter jacket. She added a hat with ear flaps, and a huge scarf.

Dad laughed. "You look like an Eskimo! But you're right, it's freezing out there. I wouldn't be surprised if it snowed soon. Now where are my gloves?"

Ella was dancing around with impatience by the time her mum and dad were ready. Dad popped next door to borrow their cat basket, and he laughed at Ella's jittery face. "Well, what were you thinking, that you'd just tuck her inside that scarf of yours?" Ella thought that sounded perfect. Finally they were ready to go, walking through town, weaving their way through the bustling shoppers. It was lovely – with Christmas only four days away, everyone was in a festive mood, and all the shop windows were full

of presents, tinsel and sparkling Christmas trees.

Ella held her dad's hand, rushing him along. "She's such a pretty kitten, Dad, you'll love her. I'll look after her really well, I promise. Oh, look, there's the sign for the farm. Come on! I can't wait to see her again!"

Ella ran the last little way, and her mum and dad exchanged smiles. They hadn't been sure about letting Ella have a kitten, but she was so happy, it had to be the right decision.

They opened the farm gate, and Ella dashed off to try and find Fluff, while her parents went to look for Mrs Moffat.

"Fluff! Fluff!" Ella called, but no little kitten came running. There was a

beautiful big tabby cat, sitting quietly on the stable door, just where Fluff had been when Ella first saw her. Ella went over to her. "You must be Fluff's mum! You have to be, your eyes are just the same. Where is she, puss? We've come to take her home!"

The tabby cat gave Ella a long look, then jumped down from the door and disappeared round the corner of the yard, walking very fast. It was almost as if Ella had upset her.

Just then Ella's mum and dad came out of the farmhouse with Mrs Moffat. "I'm really sorry," she was explaining. "It's such bad luck – really awful timing."

"Oh no! Has someone else taken Fluff home?" Ella gasped.

"N-no – not exactly," said Mrs Moffat, looking worried. "I'm afraid Fluff is lost. Some people came to see about taking her earlier this morning, and I think the boy frightened her. She jumped over the wall and disappeared. She's never even been out of the gates before! I've been searching all around, and so have Ben and Sara, but we can't find her anywhere. It's odd, she's normally such a friendly little thing, I'd have expected her to come running. We'll keep looking, of course, but—"

Ella's dad could see that Ella was about to burst into tears, and he put his arm round her. "If you find her, could you let us know?" he asked. He scribbled their phone number on a bit of paper, and handed it to Mrs Moffat.

"Couldn't we go and look for her?" Ella begged, as they left the farm. "We might find her."

"Ella, she could be a long way away by now," her mum explained. "Mrs Moffat's already looked all around here. I'm afraid we haven't got much chance of finding her."

"But she's so little! And Mrs Moffat said she's never been outside the farm before." Ella started to cry, and her dad hugged her tight.

"Mrs Moffat's going to keep looking. You never know…"

Ella nodded miserably, and shivered. It was so cold. Poor Fluff was out here lost and all alone. How would such a little kitten ever find her way home?

Chapter Six

The minute Fluff had landed on the other side of the wall, she'd set off as fast as her legs would carry her. She wanted to get as far away as possible from that horrible boy and, without knowing it, she'd run into one of the town's main streets, which was packed with Christmas shoppers. Now, Fluff was cowering behind a rubbish bin,

watching shoes, all of which were threatening to step on her. She'd been sitting there for ages. She'd never imagined that outside could be so big. There were so many people, and so many cars roaring past. No wonder Rosie had warned them to stay in the yard! She had no idea what she should do next. How on earth was she going to find Ella? Cautiously, she put a paw out of her hiding place, and then whipped it back quickly as another boot came down and nearly squashed it. She squeezed herself back behind the bin and sat there shivering.

Fluff felt like she'd been under there for hours when she finally dared to come out. She felt safer now that it was dark, and there were fewer people

about. She sniffed the air hopefully. Food smells were all around, but she had no idea where they were coming from. Back at the farm she would have been fed by now, and her stomach rumbled loudly. She slunk along the edges of the pavement, hiding in the shadows, until finally the shops gave way to houses and gardens. Then she jumped up on to a wall to give herself a view of the street, and settled down for a little rest, and a think about what to do next.

All at once she missed the cosy stable, and the comforting sound of Gus the pony snorting in his sleep. *Oh, why did I ever leave the farm?* Fluff mewed. Then she shook her whiskers firmly. *Because I'm going to find Ella, that's why,* she told herself.

Suddenly she was jolted out of her thoughts by an angry hissing. She spun round at once, her fur fluffing up. A huge tomcat was towering over her, his ginger tail flailing to and fro, and his whiskers bristling.

Fluff gasped. He seemed to be at least three times as big as she was! She mewed hopefully at him. Perhaps he could show her where to find some food. Ducking her head shyly, she crept along the wall towards him.

But the tomcat was anything but friendly. He made a low growling noise as he inched towards her. Then, in one quick movement, he lifted one of his enormous paws and cuffed Fluff round the head, sending her flying. Dazed, Fluff landed badly on the pavement

below. She shot off down the road,
looking back just once, to see the
massive cat hulking on the wall and
staring after her.

Fluff didn't stop running until she was at least three roads away. She sneaked under a gate into a garden, and wriggled herself under a bush, her heart thumping. She was only a kitten, and she had no idea about life outside the farm. How was she to know that the wall belonged to the tomcat? Did everywhere outside belong to somebody else? She tried to snuggle down into the old dead leaves under the bush, but she couldn't relax, and she spent the rest of the night dozing, and then waking in a panic every time she heard a rustle of leaves, or the squawk of a night bird. *I shouldn't have run away*, Fluff thought to herself. *Even that boy couldn't be as bad as this? Could he?*

Only a few streets away, Ella's parents were sitting in their warm kitchen drinking a cup of tea together. Ella's mum frowned. "I really don't know what to do to cheer her up," she sighed. "It's not that she's being sulky, or difficult, or anything like that – she just seems so sad."

Ella's dad nodded. "What's really upset her is that Fluff's out there lost and all alone. Ella's frightened for her."

"And I have a horrible feeling that Mrs Moffat won't be able to find her," worried Ella's mum. "I know I didn't really want Ella to have a cat, but it's so sad that it's turned out like this. It's so cold out there at the moment, and—

Goodness, what was that? Did you hear a noise out in the hall?"

They jumped up from the table and hurried out of the kitchen.

"Ella! What on earth are you doing? You're supposed to be in bed!"

Ella was standing on a pile of books, trying to undo the security chain on the front door. She was wearing her pyjamas tucked into her purple wellies, and her eyes were blotchy from crying.

"I've got to find Fluff!" she said desperately, scrabbling at the chain. "Can we go out and look for her?" The street light was casting strange blue and green shadows through the stained-glass panels in the door, and Ella looked like a little ghost.

"Ella, it's ten o'clock! And it's freezing outside!" Ella's mum started to help her down from her makeshift ladder.

"I know!" Ella wailed. "But Fluff's out there, Mum, all on her own. Please let me go out and look for her!"

"Ella, you can't go out there in the dark," said her dad firmly. "Anyway, someone else might have found Fluff; she could be fine. But I promise I'll take you out looking for her tomorrow. And Mum will ring the farm and see if they've had any more news." He tightened the security chain carefully. "That's only if you go straight back to bed now."

Ella cast one longing look back at the door, and reluctantly sat down on

the stairs to take off her wellies. "You promise?"

"Definitely. We'll do our best to find her, just not now."

Ella nodded, and trailed sadly back up the stairs, carrying her books.

Chapter Seven

Fluff woke with a start, to find that it was getting light. She shivered as she remembered why she wasn't curled up in the cosy stable with Rosie. She stretched painfully, stiff with cold, and started on a quick morning wash. It was while she was busy with the delicate job of behind her ears that she realized what the strange feeling in her

middle must be. She hadn't had anything to eat since yesterday's breakfast, and she was starving! She needed to find some food very soon. She could smell that there were mice about, but she didn't think she had much chance of catching one. But that bin she'd sheltered under yesterday had had food smells coming from it. She set off out of the garden to find a bin.

It wasn't long before she came to a litter-bin attached to a lamp-post. Fluff sniffed hopefully – it had a definite foody whiff. It took several goes, but after a flying leap, and a lot of scrabbling, Fluff found herself balanced on the edge of the bin, catching her breath. She took a deep sniff – cheese! Sara had occasionally

given her a nibble of cheese from her sandwiches, and there was definitely cheese in this bin. There was another odd smell as well, a little like mouse, but Fluff wasn't quite sure what it was.

Fluff leaned over, balancing as carefully as she could. Yes, there it was! Half a cheese sandwich! She reached out a delicate paw and hooked it out triumphantly. She was just about to jump down and drag the sandwich away somewhere quiet when there was a sudden scuffling noise underneath her, and the rubbish moved.

An enormous rat popped up from under a hamburger box, and bared his dirty great teeth at Fluff. Then he snatched the sandwich back, and hissed at her.

Fluff lost her balance and slid off backwards, twisting frantically in the air, but still landing painfully and jarring her paws. She raced off down the road, sure she could still hear the rat's horrible hissing in her ear.

At last, out of breath, and with her paws aching, she scuttled under a parked car to hide. *What am I going to do?* she panicked to herself. *I can't find anywhere safe to sleep, or anything to eat, and I can't find Ella! Maybe I should just go back?* She missed Rosie, and Gus the pony, and everyone at the farm. And right this minute, she really missed the food, and her warm bed in the stable!

The farm was the only home she'd ever known, and all she had to do was go back the way she'd come. Surely that boy would have gone by now. *Maybe they'll be glad to see me back?* she thought. *They might even let me stay!* She set off, retracing her steps, but crossing to the other side of the

road and running to avoid the litter-bin and the scary rat. Those first few streets weren't too hard, but when Fluff got back to the garden where she'd slept under a bush, nothing looked familiar. Which way had she come from? Where was the tomcat's wall? Fluff shivered with cold. She looked down the road one way, and then the other. She hadn't a clue – but it was getting so cold and she had to make a decision. She set off again, hoping that she would come across something that she remembered. But a few streets later Fluff found herself trotting past a little row of shops that she was certain she'd never seen before. She paused on the edge of the pavement to try and work out when she'd made her mistake.

Suddenly, there was a loud roaring noise and a car shot past her, skidding through a deep, muddy puddle, and soaking Fluff to the skin in dirty water. She gasped in shock as she felt the cold biting into her. She shuddered, and looked round desperately for a warm place to dry off.

A lady with a big shopping bag was going into one of the shops, and Fluff felt the gust of warmth as the door opened. *Surely they wouldn't mind if I just went in to get warm,* she thought to herself. *I won't stay long.*

The shop was brightly lit, and it looked so inviting that Fluff couldn't resist. She hurried over and followed the lady in, sneaking along behind her shopping bag.

It was so nice to be somewhere warm again! She peeped around the side of the bag, and gulped with delight. There was a bowl of food at the corner of the counter! Fluff didn't stop to think. She darted over to the bowl and started to gobble as fast as she could.

She'd managed a few mouthfuls, when a strange rrrrr-ing noise made the fur on the back of her neck lift up. She froze in panic, her heart thumping. There wasn't a dog on the farm, and Fluff had never met one before, but some deep cat instinct stirred inside her.

The rrrrr-ing changed to a deep woof, and suddenly an enormous creature flung itself at Fluff, barking madly and baring its teeth.

The lady with the bag and the shop-owner looked down in amazement. "What's the matter with you, Fergus, you daft dog? Oh my goodness! Where did that scrawny little thing come from? And it's stealing your dinner! Shoo, you nasty stray. Go on, Fergus, chase it out, it's probably full of fleas!" The man flung the door open and Fergus (who was only a dachshund, but thought he was at least a Great Dane) chased Fluff out on to the pavement, his teeth only inches from her tail.

When Fluff dared to look back, she was surprised to see that the dog wasn't actually much bigger than she was. It wasn't fair! Why shouldn't she have had some of that nice food too? There had been plenty for them both. She skidded

to a stop and spat angrily at Fergus. She was sick of running away. She stood nose to nose with the little dog and snarled, her tail twitching. Then as he started to bark again, she shot out a paw and raked her tiny claws down his muzzle.

Fergus howled with shock. The little cat was supposed to run off shaking like a jelly, not fight back! He wailed again, and his owner, who'd been watching from the door, flung a newspaper at Fluff, yelling, "Get out of here, you horrible stray!"

Fluff dodged the newspaper, but the man's words hit her. She'd been too busy running the first time he'd called her a stray, but now it struck home. She slunk off into the shadows, feeling more alone than ever. She was a stray!

She knew all about strays. No one wanted them, and Rosie chased them away if they came to the farm. If Fluff was a stray cat now, maybe she wouldn't be welcome at the farm after all...

Chapter Eight

Fluff padded sadly along the pavement. She was a little less hungry after the food she'd stolen from Fergus's bowl, but she was still frozen. It was already getting dark again, and it seemed even colder than the night before. Fluff decided to look for somewhere to hide for the night, and think about what to do in the morning.

She trotted down a dark alleyway, with a row of bins down one side.

The alley was full of good smells, but about halfway down Fluff noticed another smell that somehow wasn't so good. In fact, it was almost a scary smell. She took a deep sniff, trying to work out what it was. It was a little bit like the smell of Fergus, but not quite. Stronger and – dirtier, somehow… She lifted her head, sensing that someone was watching her, and gulped.

A huge fox was peering at her round the nearest rubbish bin, his tongue lolling, and a hungry gleam in his eye. He had Fluff cornered, and they both knew it.

Fluff froze in panic for a second. He was enormous!

Then she shot backwards, and
squeezed herself into a tiny space
between two bins, where the fox
wouldn't be able to get in. Did foxes

eat kittens? Fluff wasn't sure, but this one was looking at her as though she might make a tasty snack. He stuck his nose into Fluff's hidey-hole, eyeing her all the while. Then he scrabbled a paw in, and then his shoulder, and then he barged one of the bins out of the way, knocking it over. He grinned at Fluff, showing his enormous teeth.

Fluff was trapped, but she wasn't giving up. She'd seen off Fergus, hadn't she? She fluffed up her fur and hissed defiantly, as much to make herself feel brave as anything else. The fox crept closer, and Fluff batted at it angrily with one tiny paw. It was like hitting a rock. This was no Fergus, about to turn tail. But there was nothing else she could do...

Fluff hissed and spat as well as she knew how, and amazingly, after a few seconds the fox stopped. He seemed confused. He put his head on one side, and watched her, a puzzled look in his eyes. Then, slowly, he started to make a strange barking noise, and crouched down with his long muzzle resting on his paws.

Fluff gazed at him, confused and scared. What was he doing? It sounded almost like – was he laughing at her? She edged as far back as she could into the shelter of the bins, not sure what to do next. The fox watched, his nose still on his paws, and gave an encouraging yap. Then he wriggled backwards on his haunches, giving her a clear space to escape.

Fluff watched, puzzled. Was he not going to eat her after all? He looked almost friendly. Suddenly the fox sprang up, and Fluff squashed herself backwards against the wall, trembling. But instead of launching himself at the bin, the fox turned tail and disappeared off down the alley. Fluff waited a moment, then poked her nose gingerly out of her hiding place, and peered

round. The fox was coming back, his white-tipped tail waving jauntily, and in his mouth was a piece of ham. It was chewed and smelly, but it looked delicious. Fluff's whiskers twitched with longing.

The fox laid the ham down in front of Fluff, and retreated.

Was this a trap? Was he going to pounce as soon as she was out of her shelter? Fluff eyed the ham, and tried to measure the distances. But her tummy was telling her to forget being careful and go for the food! She darted swiftly out, grabbed the ham and ran back to the bins. The fox just watched, making that odd barking noise again. He hadn't even tried to catch her. Maybe he was friendly? Fluff shivered.

This was the first friendly creature she'd met since she left the farm. It seemed strange that it should be a huge, scary fox.

The fox disappeared again, and Fluff watched eagerly this time. Was he going to get more food? The fox trotted back, holding something in his mouth carefully. He set it down gently, and pushed it towards her – a half-full tin of tuna! This time Fluff didn't hesitate. The smell of the fish was too good to resist. The fox watched admiringly as Fluff wolfed it down, licking the edges of the tin to catch the last morsels.

As Fluff licked the delicious juice from her whiskers, a huge yawn overtook her, and she stretched. Now

that she wasn't so hungry, she realized how tired she was. But she still had nowhere to sleep.

The fox watched her thoughtfully, head on one side. Then he gave an encouraging yap, and jerked his head. Fluff looked back cautiously. He seemed to want her to follow him. She wasn't sure whether it was safe, but she was just so tired. Perhaps the fox was going to show her somewhere she could rest. She set off after the fox, too sleepy to worry any more. He led her off down the alley, looking back every so often to nod and twitch his ears at her.

They scrabbled under a fence – it was much easier for Fluff than it was for the fox – and into an overgrown

garden. The fox threaded his way through the brambles, and then stood back proudly. He'd brought her to his den! It was a comfy hole under a garden shed, and it smelled horribly of fox. But Fluff was in no position to be choosy. The fox gave her a gentle nudge with his long nose, and she crept inside, snuggling down into an old sack. The fox looked in after her, as if to check she was all right, and then trotted off. Fluff guessed he was going to find his own food.

Despite the smell, Fluff slept until it was light. Then she woke and stretched sleepily, confused for a moment about where she was. Of course! The fox's hole! And it looked as though he'd left her a snack. Lying by her nose was a

bit of old kipper. Fluff nibbled it gratefully, still wondering why the fox had turned out to be so friendly. She stuck her nose out from under the shed and sniffed the fresh morning air. It was a nice change after the foxy whiff of the den. After a good sleep, and something to eat, Fluff was feeling much better. She was sure she would find Ella today. She wished the fox had come back so she could say goodbye, but there was no sign of him.

But if I don't find Ella, she thought, *I'll have no trouble finding my way back to see the fox again. I'll just follow the smell!*

Chapter Nine

"So, no news then?" Ella's mum said into the phone. Ella sat on the kitchen worktop beside her, desperately trying to hear what Mrs Moffat was saying. "No, it's awful, isn't it? Ella and her dad went out yesterday looking for Fluff, all around the town. They were out for hours, but they didn't even find anyone who'd spotted her. Well, thanks for

trying, and do let us know if you hear anything." She put the phone down. "They haven't seen her, I'm afraid. Don't look so sad, Ella, someone else might have found her! She could be having a lovely breakfast right this minute. Which reminds me – eat some of yours."

"I'm not hungry," Ella said sadly, as she went back to her breakfast and started pushing her Rice Krispies round the bowl. "Can we go out and put up the posters I made of Fluff?"

"Yes. *When* you've eaten your breakfast," her mother added, as Ella leaped down from the worktop.

Ella sat down and started to shovel in her cereal as fast as she could.

"And always assuming you haven't

choked to death on a Rice Krispie," her mother sighed.

They walked over towards the farm to start with, and then came back along the main street. It was another freezing cold day, and even Ella was starting to flag after an hour of sticking posters of Fluff on to every lamp-post they could find. They all said the same thing:

Several people stopped to look and say how cute the little kitten was, but no one had seen her. When they got to the playground, a few streets from their house, Ella's mum persuaded her to call it a day. "Lots of people will see all those posters. We need to get back home before we freeze. Come on, we'll go home and have some hot chocolate to warm us up. And then you promised to help me sort out all that old junk in the garage, remember?"

Ella nodded sadly. She'd really hoped that they would spot Fluff, but there'd been no sign of her. Ella tucked the roll of Sellotape back into her pocket, and put her gloves on. Her hands were going numb, and she shivered. Poor little Fluff. Mum and

Dad kept saying that someone had probably found her by now, but what if she was still out in the cold?

Fluff was outside, and she was frozen. She'd set out from the fox's den that morning feeling very confident, but an hour later, she was running out of energy. She plodded on, her paws starting to feel tired again, and then, at the end of the road, she heard a noise that gave her some hope. She broke into a run, and rounded the corner, following the laughter and yells to a playground. A group of children, all wearing winter coats and scarves, were rushing about madly to keep warm.

Fluff crouched down by the gate, searching the faces for Ella, but there was no sign of her. As she watched, still more children arrived. It seemed that every child in the neighbourhood was coming and going from the playground. So surely Ella would come there too? She settled herself under one of the benches round the edge of the playground, and prepared to keep watch. Some of the children tried to coax her out, but she wouldn't come. One little girl reached under to pat her, but her mother grabbed her, and told her off. "Leave it, Lucy, it's a stray. Look how dirty and matted its fur is. Don't encourage it!"

Several times she got up, ready to rush over to some dark-haired girl

muffled up in a coat and hat, and then realized at the last minute that it wasn't Ella. But it wasn't until it began to get dark, and the parents sitting around waiting for their children started to call to them to go home, that Fluff was forced to give up. She felt sure she'd find Ella here – she'd never seen so many children before. She left the playground, following the last of the children, and wandered down the road, trying to think what to do. She didn't know that there was a poster with her picture pinned to every lamp-post.

She was hungry again, and thirsty, so she slipped under a garden gate, and started to look around. The third garden she came to had a birdbath. Fluff leaped up on to the edge and

dipped her tongue in. The water was freezing – really freezing, for the edges of the birdbath were icing over. Fluff shivered as she felt the icy water settling in her tummy, and then jumped as something cold landed on her nose. Snow! Fluff had never seen it before, but Rosie had told her about it. She leaped down on to the grass, and couldn't resist jumping and batting at the thick white flakes for a while, but the snow was falling fast, and soon her paws were soaked.

Fluff looked uncertainly towards the house. The windows were brightly lit, and she watched as two children hung up tinsel round the pictures on the walls. There was a plump black cat with them, perched comfortably on the back of the sofa. Fluff could almost hear it purring. She jumped up on to the window sill, which was already coated with a layer of snow, and pressed herself against the glass, desperate to be inside the warm room. The little boy went out, and came back with a sandwich, which he shared with the black cat! Fluff could hardly bear to watch, and she mewed piteously, hoping he would notice her, and let her have some too. But no one heard her. Then the children started a game,

wafting the tinsel around for the cat to
chase, but all it did was yawn, and put
out a paw occasionally.

"I'll chase it," Fluff mewed. "I'll chase it for you properly!" But still they took no notice, and then their mother came in, and drew the curtains, to shut out the dark and cold. No one saw the little brown cat, huddled on the window sill, crying to be let in.

Fluff jumped down, and set off again. She needed to find shelter, out of the snow. In the short time she'd spent on the window sill, those few flakes of snow had thickened to a storm, and the snow already covered her paws as she plodded wearily through it. *I'll find a shed to hide under until this stops*, she decided. But none of the sheds had space to wriggle underneath them like her fox friend's den. She tried hiding behind some bins

down the side of a house, but the wind whistled straight through, and it was almost colder than out in the open.

She ducked underneath another fence, and tracked across the next garden. The house was brightly lit, and the lamplight shining through the curtains cast pretty shadows through the blue and green stained glass in the door. *There's probably another fat black cat in there,* Fluff thought sadly. *Probably having its tea.* There were cardboard boxes by the garage, all piled up. One was full of old newspapers, and Fluff looked at it thoughtfully. It wasn't a great place to shelter, but there wasn't much snow on it, and the newspapers did look so comfortable… Perhaps she could just have a little rest?

She clambered in, her legs feeling awkward and clumsy with the cold, and curled up, a tiny ball of damp fur. She hadn't meant to go to sleep, but she was so tired. The snow kept falling, and it wasn't long before even the tips of Fluff's ears were covered. But by then, Fluff had fallen into a deep, cold sleep...

Chapter Ten

Ella had been watching from the window for her dad for nearly an hour by the time he came home.

"Sorry I'm late, sweetheart, there was loads to finish up before the Christmas holiday," he explained as he hugged her.

"Did you see her, Dad? While you were driving home, did you see Fluff?"

"No, Ella, I'm sorry. You didn't have any luck when you went out looking with Mum today, then?"

"No." Ella shook her head sadly. "We went all round, as far as the playground, but we didn't see her. We put Lost posters up everywhere, too, with pictures I drew of Fluff on them."

"Well, we'll go out and look again tomorrow. It's Christmas Eve, and I'll be home all day. Good thing too, the snow's getting quite deep out there."

Ella's mum called from the kitchen, "Is that you, Dave? Don't take your shoes off yet!"

Ella's dad sighed. "What is it? Can't it wait until tomorrow, it's freezing out there! Can't I have a cup of tea and a sit-down?" he called.

"No, because then I'll never get you out again! Ella and I sorted out all that recycling in the garage this afternoon; it took us ages. And now it's outside the garage getting snowed on! Can you put it in the car for me, so we're ready next time we go past the recycling bins?"

"OK, OK," Ella's dad grumbled. He wound his scarf back round his neck, and stepped out into the cold. He hurried over to the pile of boxes, leaving deep footprints in the snow. "They're full of snow already," he called back to Ella, who was peering round the door. "And heavy – ugh!" He picked up one of the boxes and struggled down the path to the car, balancing it on one knee while he unlocked the

boot. It took a few trips, but at last he headed back to the house, looking forward to a nice hot cup of tea.

Ella sat at the kitchen table, watching him drink it and looking hopeful. "Ella, it's no good you giving me that look. I'm not taking you out to search for Fluff again now. It's dark!"

"But Dad, you said the snow's getting deep! What if poor Fluff's buried in it?"

Her dad sighed. "Ella. I'm sorry, but if that's the case, then we wouldn't be able to find her, would we? I'm sure someone else will have found her by now. You've put the posters up, so maybe whoever found her will get in touch." He knew that actually it wasn't very likely, but he was desperate to cheer her up. "You know what? I've just remembered that I've got a surprise for you in the car! Come and see!"

"What's the surprise, Dad?" Ella asked as they trekked down the path, trying hard to sound excited. But he only smiled and wouldn't tell her. "Look on the back seat."

As she opened the car door and peered into the back seat, she heard an odd rustling sound from the boot. "Dad? Does my surprise make a noise?"

"What, love?" Ella's dad was stamping his feet to keep warm.

"There was a funny noise from the boot. Is it the surprise?"

"There's nothing in the boot except those boxes of newspapers and things that you and your mum sorted out. It was probably just some snow falling off the roof, or something."

"I'm sure it came from the boot," Ella said doubtfully. She climbed in and peered over the back seat but the parcel shelf was fixed in the way. The rustling sound came again, and Ella jumped, bumping her head on the car roof. "Ow! Dad, I heard it again! There is something in the boot, honestly." Ella wriggled out backwards, feeling a bit nervous. "There's something moving about! Have you got a torch?"

"Well, there's a torch in the glove compartment, but really, Ella, there's nothing there!" He reached into the front of the car and scrabbled around for the torch. "There you go."

Back in the boot, Fluff was stirring. Ella's dad had had the heater on while he was driving home from work, and

the car was still quite warm. Warmer than Fluff had been all day. She stretched blissfully in her sleep, and the melting snow slid off her, just as Ella opened the boot and shone the torch inside.

"Wh—! Fluff! Oh, Dad, look, Fluff's in the box! That's the surprise; you've found Fluff! But you told me you hadn't seen her!"

"What? I haven't! My surprise was a big box of chocolates!" Her dad looked confused. "Are you sure?" He peered into the boot. "Well, that's definitely a kitten… How on earth did she get there? You're sure that's Fluff?"

"I'm sure! Oh, Dad, she came to find us, and she went to sleep in the box!" Gently, Ella reached in and lifted the snoozing kitten out. "Oh, she's all wet and freezing! We have to get her dry."

Ella's dad shook his head. "I can't believe she came looking for you. Come on, let's get her inside in the warm."

They rushed back to the house, and into the kitchen. Ella's mum was cooking the dinner, and didn't look round. "So what was the surprise?

Chocolates, perhaps? I could just do with a chocolate."

"Oh! We left them in the car!" Ella giggled, sounding happy for the first time in days. "Sorry, Mum!"

"Mmm, and I've got a complaint, Jen. You said you'd sorted through all that recycling," said Ella's dad, grinning. "Those bins are for bottles and paper only, you know. No kittens allowed."

"What?" Ella's mum spun round and saw Fluff cuddled in Ella's arms. "Oh! I don't believe it! Is that really Fluff? Where was she?"

"In amongst those newspapers, in the boot of the car!"

Fluff was staring blearily around, wondering if she was still dreaming.

But the soft towel that the girl was rubbing her with seemed to be real, and the girl really was Ella! She managed a small purr as the warmth started to seep into her bones.

"We haven't any cat food," said Ella's mum worriedly, opening the kitchen cupboard. "Do you think she'd like tuna?" she said, holding out a tin to Ella. Fluff recognised it at once, and stood up shakily on Ella's lap, mewing hopefully.

"Mmm, well, I'd better find the tin-opener." Ella's mum shook her head in amazement. "I just can't believe we found her!"

"She found us, Mum! It's like a Christmas wish come true." Ella smiled to herself, stroking Fluff's ears. *And we're Fluff's Christmas present*, she thought. *Fluff's got a home for Christmas.*

"We should call the farm and let them know," Ella's dad said, as he

searched for an old bowl to put Fluff's tuna in.

"But Dad, what if they want her back?" Ella gasped in horror, and hugged Fluff tightly, making her squeak. "Sorry, Fluff!"

"Don't worry, Ella. I'm sure they'll be delighted for you to keep her. They know how much you wanted Fluff and that you'll take good care of her." Her mum crouched down next to her and tickled Fluff under the chin. "You're right, she's not grubby, she's gorgeous!" She grinned at Ella, remembering the first time she'd seen Fluff. "We just don't want everyone at the farm to worry any more, that's all. Mrs Moffat wanted a good home for Fluff, and now she's got one."

Ella nodded, relieved. "And you'd better remind Mrs Moffat to tell Fluff's mum she's safe. She was really worried." She saw her mum and dad exchange an amused look over her head, but she didn't care. Fluff was home, and nothing else mattered. And Fluff, tucking into the big bowl of tuna, thought so too.

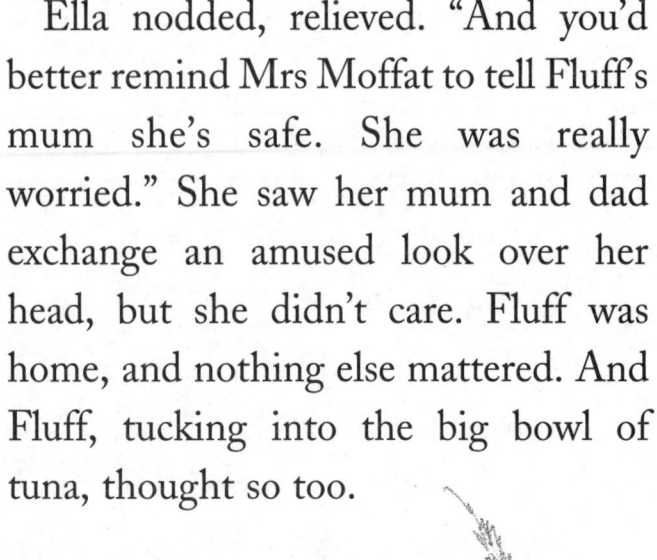